# Alex AND THE ALPACAS
## SAVE THE WORLD

*For Khrob. Of course.*

# Alex AND THE ALPACAS SAVE THE WORLD

## KATHRYN LEFROY

 FREMANTLE PRESS

# CHAPTER ONE

As the sleek silver car hurtled along the deserted highway, Alex buzzed the window down and sucked in huge lungfuls of dawn air. Up until this second, she'd never understood why people said country air smelled different. But this air was nothing like the city — this air was the ocean and the forest and the promise of adventure.

Yesterday, she'd been staring down the barrel of the most boring summer holiday known to humankind. This was to include such thrilling activities as: waiting for Mum to get home from work, avoiding the phone in case it was Dad, and pretending to be totally enthralled by her friends' updates from Bali or Disneyland — or wherever else proper families went on holiday.

And, okay, fine, Alex would be the first to admit that a farm in the middle of Tasmania wasn't as good as some fancy resort that had seven waterslides and drinks with umbrellas in them. But at least farms had horses to ride, baby animals to feed, and homemade cakes to eat. And on a scale of homework to drinks with umbrellas, those things were definitely closer to drinks with umbrellas.

Out her window, Alex watched while rolling hills, green as apples, tumbled away into the distance. As the rising sun caught beads of morning dew, the whole world seemed to sparkle. While the rest of Australia coughed and wheezed its way through the driest summer on record, Tasmania felt fresh and exciting. Alex grinned. Yep, this holiday was going to be great.

'Alex, come on,' Mum said with a tired sigh, not taking her eyes off the road. 'Close the window. It's freezing.'

Alex gave Mum a sidelong glance but didn't argue. Mum had been weird and distracted ever since yesterday, when Uncle Neil had called with the news. Alex's Grandpa Jacob had broken his leg and needed help. And Uncle Neil couldn't just cancel the family holiday to Europe that had been planned for the last six months. So it had fallen to Mum to take time off work and head to the farm.

To Alex, Grandpa Jacob was nothing more than a faded photograph in Mum's study. A man who leaned against a tree, shirtsleeves rolled up to his elbows, and squinted into the camera lens with a not-quite smile on his face. Uncle Neil and his family went to the farm every year but an invitation hadn't ever been extended to Mum and Alex. At some point Alex had stopped asking why.

But in the last couple of days, that seemed to have changed.

They drove in silence until Mum turned onto a narrow dirt road. Alex pressed her nose against the window. 'Are we here? Is this it?'

Mum nodded. 'Just at the end of this lane.'

After bumping along the dirt track for an agonisingly long time, they finally stopped in front of a metal gate. A large hand-painted sign declared 'No Trespassers!'. Behind that, chaotic clusters of bushes guarded the edges of a long driveway, which led to a sprawling wooden house. The building might have once been blue, but was now a washed-out grey. To the left was a huge paddock that was the right size for horses, but seemed completely empty. And behind that, thick, inky forest stretched back and back and back.

'You sure this is it?' Alex asked.

'I did warn you not to get your hopes up,' Mum said. 'I haven't seen the place for over a decade. And Grandpa Jacob is —'

'Difficult. Yeah, yeah. You've said that a million times. But … I thought he'd at least have horses.'

Mum raised an eyebrow. 'You did? Why?'

Alex did not say because farms in movies always have horses. Mum was all about reason and logic, and Alex knew her assumption was based on neither of those things. 'I just thought he would,' she said.

'I can always call your dad and —'

'I am *not* staying with Isaac!' Alex spat her dad's name

out. 'He doesn't want me there, remember?'

'He didn't mean it like that,' Mum said, just as she had ten, twenty, thirty times before. 'He was just worried you'd be bored with the new baby around.'

Yeah. Right. If he meant that he would have said that.

'I'm just saying it's still an option,' Mum added. 'If you change your mind.'

'I'm not going to change my mind,' Alex said. Horses or no horses, summer on her grandfather's farm had to be better than being somewhere she wasn't wanted. She pulled up the hood of her jumper then shoved the car door wide before Mum could see the hot tears prickling the corners of her eyes. 'I'll open the gate.'

The gate was sturdy — maybe the only thing about this whole place that looked like it'd survive a strong wind — and was held closed by a rusted chain looped around a shoulder-high wooden post.

As she was edging the chain over the top Alex noticed the post had some kind of pattern carved into it. Age had worn away at the design so it was only a whisper in the splintery timber. She peered closer. A chunky cross surrounded by a circle. Inside the circle, at the end of each arm of the cross, was a small triangle, pointy side facing out. And right at the centre of the cross was another circle.

She traced the pattern with her finger. Some kind of symbol perhaps? Whatever it was, it looked old. Really old. She felt a sudden, sharp sting and snatched her hand back. A splinter was wedged into her fingertip. 'Great,' she muttered, squeezing until she could ease the shard of wood out. She shoved her finger in her mouth, trying to suck the ache away, and scowled at the symbol and the drop of her blood that had left a tiny dark stain on the wooden post.

From somewhere up the hill, far past the house, a breath of wind rustled a pocket of trees in the forest. The noise wasn't loud, but it was constant. Like the forest sighing. Distracted from her throbbing finger, Alex looked towards the sound.

A tunnel of wind burst from the edge of the forest. It rushed across the grass and down the hill. The plants and trees in its path shuddered and swayed, a line of vicious movement through the otherwise still landscape, which seemed to be heading straight for Alex. A prickle ran the length of Alex's spine. Wind couldn't go in a straight line like that … could it?

Then the wind was right there, wrapping around her in a swirling vault, icy as the ocean in winter, musty as a forgotten tomb. The hood of Alex's jumper flipped off and her ponytail flicked around her face.

And then the wind whispered into her ear, a hiss so low that Alex might have imagined the words. Except she did not.

*Ready or not. Here I come …*

# Chapter Two

Alex's pulse thudded. She wanted to run, but she was too terrified to move.

'Alex? What are you doing?'

The sound of Mum's voice snapped her back to reality.

Alex didn't waste any time as she wrenched the rusty gate open and raced back to the car. She slammed then locked the door. Her teeth chattered. 'Did you see that?'

'See what?' Mum put the car into drive and edged carefully through the gate.

'That wind. It came straight out of the forest at me.' Alex peered out the window. Everything was still again, the morning sky clear and blue. Like nothing strange had happened at all. 'It was sort of like a … tornado thing.' It wasn't, but she couldn't think of a better way to describe it.

'It's just the wind.' Mum pulled the car up to the front of the house and switched off the engine.

\*\*\*

Grandpa Jacob's front door was a monstrous slab of dark wood surrounded by stained glass. Mum rapped tentatively on the wood.

No answer.

She tried again.

Still nothing. Taking a deep breath, Mum gave three solid thumps that echoed through the depths of the house. A voice shouted back, 'I'm coming, I'm coming. Hold y'horses!'

Uneven footsteps became louder and louder, then stopped. Without realising she was doing it, Alex edged closer to Mum.

The door opened. Grandpa Jacob in real life was an older, more hollowed-out version of the photo from Mum's study. His hair was a heavy swirl of dark brown, and his eyes were cool and grey. On his right leg was a moon boot cast.

The old man's face registered confusion, then surprise. 'Is that … Elina?'

'Hi Dad.'

He peered at her. 'You look different.'

Mum gave him a too-bright smile. 'Ten years, three jobs, a child and a divorce will do that.'

'What are you doing here?' He opened the door wider and glanced behind Mum. 'Where's Neil? And Wilfred?'

'They're on their way to Europe,' Mum explained, patiently, like she was talking to a kid. 'Neil told you that. Alex and I came instead.'

'Hi.' Alex gave her grandfather a shy smile.

It was not returned. In fact, he barely even looked at her. 'You and Alice came instead?' he repeated. 'Instead of Wilfred?'

Alex tried not to let the sting show on her face. Grandpa Jacob thought she was called *Alice*? She was nothing like an Alice! And why would he rather spend the summer with her gaming-obsessed cousin, Wilfred? Alex could hardly imagine Wilfred wanting to *visit* a farm, let alone spend the *whole summer* on one. Unless it was a farm in a video game. With zombies. That he had to blow up.

'It's *Alex*, not Alice,' Mum corrected, mouth tight. 'And yes. We came instead of Wilfred and Neil.'

The confusion on Grandpa Jacob's face morphed into anger. 'So he lied to me? Neil lied to me?'

Alex's eyebrows shot up. Wait a second. Grandpa Jacob didn't even know she and Mum were coming? No wonder he was acting so strange.

'It wasn't a lie,' Mum said slowly, 'Neil *told* you that I would come instead —'

'And I told him that wouldn't do,' Grandpa Jacob said. 'I told him I had fractured my foot and needed him and Wilfred. And he said he would arrange to help me for the summer.'

Mum held up her arms in a sort of surrender. 'And here we are. The help that's been arranged.'

'This is … this is … unacceptable!' Grandpa Jacob blustered. He turned and limped hurriedly down the hall, the cast on his foot banging against the floorboards with each step.

Alex leaned to Mum and whispered, 'He seriously didn't know we were coming?'

Mum made a face halfway between a smile and a grimace and didn't answer. That was a definite no. Alex opened her mouth to tell Mum how unfair that was — to him *and* her — but she hadn't got a single word out before Mum gave her an imploring look and nudged her inside. *Not now. Please.*

So Alex shut her mouth and followed behind her grandfather as he thumped his way down the hall.

At the end of the hallway was a large, bright kitchen. A wooden table commanded the centre of the room, and in the corner an ancient fridge rumbled noisily. A single mug and spoon were in the sink, and they rattled as Grandpa Jacob stomped across the kitchen in a beeline for the phone.

'Did the doctors say it's okay for you to be walking?' Mum asked.

He snorted as he picked up the phone. 'What am I meant to do instead? Fly?'

He dialled a number and his fingers drummed a frenetic rhythm as he waited for the other end to answer. Nothing. He hung up, then tried again. And again. And again.

'They're on a plane, Dad,' Mum said. Her patience was straining. 'Would it be so bad if we stayed to help out with the farm? I'm sure there's nothing they could do that we couldn't.'

He puffed up his chest, indignant. 'I don't need help with the farm!'

Mum suppressed a groan. 'Then why is it so important that Neil and Wilfred are here?'

Grandpa Jacob didn't say anything immediately, but then he shook his head. 'You wouldn't understand.' He hobbled to a cupboard and took out a large, colourful plate. 'I need to feed the alpacas. Kettle's over there if you want tea.'

'Alpacas?' Mum frowned. 'I didn't know you had alpacas.'

'They turned up, oh, nine or ten years ago, and never left,' Grandpa Jacob said gruffly. 'And they don't like it when I'm late with their breakfast.'

'Alex, why don't you go with Grandpa Jacob to feed the alpacas?' Mum said, using her fake-happy voice. 'That sounds fun, doesn't it?'

Alex and her grandfather eyed each other, wary. While Alex was slightly buoyed by the idea of alpacas (they weren't horses but they were better than nothing), she did not agree with her mum's assessment that feeding them with him was going to be 'fun'.

From the expression on Grandpa Jacob's face, neither did he.

But Mum nudged Alex's shoulder and gave her such a desperate pleading look that Alex didn't have the heart to disagree.

'Yeah,' she said. 'That'd be great.'

Grandpa Jacob selected four apples from a fruit bowl. He deftly cut them into slices and put them on the colourful plate. He looked at Alex. 'Well? Are you coming or not?'

# CHAPTER THREE

Alex silently followed her grandfather as he stomped down the back path. When she was younger, she'd often quizzed Mum about why they'd never been to visit Grandpa Jacob when Uncle Neil and his family did every year. Mum always offered the same vague explanation that she and Grandpa Jacob had drifted apart over the years. It had never made sense to Alex before.

But having spent all of ten minutes with her grandfather she was starting to get it. It wasn't that different from her own dad and her new sister. Half-sister, she reminded herself. Not even a real sister. Dad had cancelled Alex's summer plans to visit him because his new daughter was more important to him than his old one. Her own dad had his favourite kid. It seemed Grandpa Jacob did as well. And it wasn't Mum.

At the end of the path, there was a gate that connected the back garden to an orchard. Alex peered curiously at the wild and overgrown trees.

'What kind of fruit are they?' she asked. She hoped his

answer would be cherries. Plums or nectarines would also be good. Or oranges at a pinch, but they weren't her favourite.

'Olives,' Grandpa Jacob said.

Alex sagged in disappointment. She hated olives.

Grandpa Jacob unlocked the latch to the gate. A faded sign attached to the wood with brass screws read, 'This Olive Grove Belongs to Rosa Surya Ortiz'.

Alex's eyebrows shot up. 'I didn't know Grandma Rosa's middle name was Surya.' Her grandmother had died soon after Alex was born.

'Her maiden name,' Grandpa Jacob replied without looking back. 'It means sun.'

Surya was Alex's middle name, too. She'd been aware that it was an old family name from her mum's side, but hadn't known it was her grandmother's surname before she got married. She didn't bother telling Grandpa Jacob any of this, though. Given that he didn't even know her first name, Alex doubted he would care.

Even with his fractured foot, Grandpa Jacob weaved easily between the grey trunks of the olive trees, ducking beneath overgrown branches heavy with waxy leaves and small green fruit. Alex stumbled after him, trying not to trip over the roots poking through the uneven ground.

On the other side of the grove was the paddock that Alex had seen on the way in. There was a wooden barn, but no sign of any alpacas. Grandpa Jacob ducked under the wire fence and Alex followed him. She was halfway through when she noticed a mark on one of the wooden posts. That ancient-looking symbol again, the same as the one she'd seen on the way in. 'What does this mean?'

Grandpa Jacob gave her a sharp look. 'It's no concern of yours.'

'There's one by the front gate, too.'

'And I said it's no concern of yours,' he repeated.

She wondered fleetingly if she should ask him about the strange wind that had started after she touched the symbol by the gate, but either he wouldn't believe her or he'd just tell her again that it wasn't any of her business. She wasn't sure which would be worse.

He handed the plate of apples to her. 'Don't break this,' he warned. Then he held his hand flat, fingers tight together, and placed a single slice of fruit in the middle of his palm. 'This is how you feed the alpacas. One piece at a time. They won't bite on purpose, but sometimes they get a bit excited and will accidentally take a nip. Ready?'

Before Alex had a chance to answer, he let out a piercing whistle that made her jump.

A midnight-black alpaca poked its head out of the barn.

'Wait for it, wait for it,' Grandpa Jacob muttered, 'three, two, one …'

The alpaca let out a delighted squawk, and thundered towards them. Close on its heels was a caramel-coloured alpaca, then a chocolate-brown one, and finally a white animal with a slash of black fur across its eyes like a mask.

Alex took a hurried step back and Grandpa Jacob let out a short laugh. The alpacas skidded to a halt in front of her, eyes glued to the fruit plate. The black one had a trail of saliva hanging from its mouth.

Grandpa Jacob rubbed each animal on the forehead, making cooing noises, then pulled seeds from the caramel alpaca's coat. 'You've been rolling in the hay again, haven't you girl,' he said affectionately. 'I'll have to bring the brush down next time.'

Alex gave him a sidelong glance. So he was capable of being nice. Just not to actual people.

'I'm going to get them some fresh water,' Grandpa Jacob said, and he stomped away, leaving Alex alone with the alpacas.

Alex eyed the animals warily. Their bodies came up to about her armpit, but because of their long giraffe-like necks they stood a full head taller than her. Strands of hay were stuck into the tight ringlets of wool that covered them from head to foot, and they smelled a bit like a damp winter coat.

The trail of saliva hanging out of the black animal's mouth was a slick thread that glistened in the sun. The alpaca sucked it back up, and then sent a huge glob of iridescent spit flying through the air. Alex screwed up her nose.

*Gross.*

Balancing the plate on one hand, she held out a slice of apple like Grandpa Jacob had shown her. The black alpaca got in first and slurped up the fruit, leaving a trail of sticky, grass-flecked saliva on her palm.

*Ugh. So gross.*

Alex wiped her hand on her jeans, glaring at the black alpaca. The animal finished its mouthful in about two seconds and when no more apple was immediately forthcoming, proceeded to help itself by sticking its face straight into the plate of fruit.

'Hey!' Alex tried to back away, but the alpaca followed her. The other alpacas nudged in, trying to get at the fruit too, jostling her roughly from side to side. She lifted the plate above her head. A woolly foot came down hard on her sneaker and she squealed. 'Ahh! Watch it!'

'If she handed over the apple, she wouldn't get hurt!' an indignant voice grumbled.

Alex spun around, looking for Grandpa Jacob. He was standing about ten feet away, peering at a tree in the grove. 'What did you say?'

He glanced over. 'Me? Nothing.'

'I thought you said —*oof!*' She stumbled forward. The chocolate alpaca was trying to get at the apple by putting its head over her arm. Alex pivoted on the spot, twisting away from the animal.

'Ouch!' It was a different voice. Female. Annoyed. 'The girl flicked me in the eye with her mane!'

Alex dropped the plate. 'What's going on?' Her voice was high-pitched, uncertain.

'What?' Grandpa Jacob limped back toward her.

The alpacas shoved Alex out of the way as they dived down, inhaling the rest of the apple in about three seconds flat.

'There were … I heard …' She glared at him. 'Is this some kind of joke?'

Grandpa Jacob saw the plate lying on the ground. It had broken in half. 'That was Rosa's favourite!'

Alex wasn't listening to him. She spun around, looking for who had spoken. But there was no one else around. 'I heard voices,' she said, quietly.

Another voice, whispering. 'Did she just say she heard voices?'

Alex felt a nudge at her elbow and whirled around to face the chocolate alpaca. The animal opened its mouth. The voice that emanated from the creature was female, and full of surprise.

'You can understand us?'

# Chapter Four

Alex half-ran, half-stumbled back through the olive grove, her thoughts tumbling around like a skydiver without a parachute.

The alpacas had talked to her.

The *alpacas* had *talked* to her.

The alpacas had talked to *her*.

And all the while her mind was screaming, 'That's not possible! Alpacas can't talk!'

She almost slammed straight into Mum, who was standing just inside the gate, staring over the olive trees.

'We need to leave,' Alex panted. 'There's something wrong with the farm.'

'What do you mean?' She looked past Alex. 'Where's Grandpa Jacob?'

On cue, a red-faced Grandpa Jacob burst through a spray of branches, holding up the two sides of the broken plate. 'Look at this! Look what she did!' He hobbled closer and waved the china in Mum's face, his voice shaking with rage.

'She broke it!'

'I remember that plate,' Mum said, touching the pieces gently. 'Mamma used to have morning tea from it every day. A sliced apple and two fig biscuits.'

Grandpa Jacob's eye twitched and he snatched the plate out of her reach. 'The girl just threw it on the ground, like it was worthless.'

'I didn't throw it,' Alex protested. 'I heard ... there were ... the alpacas ...' She trailed off, looking to Grandpa Jacob for any indication that he knew his alpacas could talk. But he was trying to fit the broken plate back together, and paid absolutely no attention to her.

'The alpacas what?' Mum asked.

Alex hesitated. She couldn't just blurt out that the alpacas had talked to her. Mum wouldn't believe something like that in a million years. In fact, Alex wasn't even sure *she* really believed it. It had happened so quickly ... Could it have been her imagination? 'I didn't throw it,' she repeated, her voice small.

'We can fix it,' Mum said. 'Alex, why don't you help Grandpa Jacob glue the plate back together?'

'I don't need her help!' Grandpa Jacob snapped. He glared at Alex once more, then limped down the path to the back door.

Mum closed her eyes briefly. 'I swear, in a previous life he must have been a goat.'

Alex looked at Mum. 'A goat?'

'He's the most stubborn person I know,' she said, wincing as the back door slammed. 'And one of the most difficult things for stubborn people to do is admit when they need help.' Mum inhaled a long breath and let it out slowly. 'But it shows great strength of character, kiddo. Don't ever forget that.'

Alex sometimes wondered if Mum's previous life had been as a fortune cookie. 'Is he mad because Neil didn't tell him we were coming?'

'Neil did tell him,' Mum said. 'But Dad refused to accept it. He just kept going on and on about how Neil and Wilfred were the only ones that could help.' She sighed. 'Why *I* can't, I'll never know but —' she shrugged, 'that's my dad for you.'

'I don't think we should stay,' Alex said. 'He doesn't want us here. And he doesn't seem like he needs help.'

Mum shook her head. 'I'm not sure he knows what he needs anymore.'

'But —'

'Come on, Alex,' Mum said, in a voice that brooked no further argument. 'I know we haven't got off to the best start, but it'll get better.' Her voice softened, and she planted a kiss on Alex's forehead. 'I promise. Now …' She put her hands on her hips and surveyed the orchard. 'Seeing as we're here, we might as well make ourselves useful. How about we start with pruning these olive trees?'

Mum marched to the back shed and flung open the doors. She rummaged through and handed Alex a pair of green-handled gardening shears. 'I used to help Mamma prune when I was your age,' Mum said. 'She called it giving the trees a haircut.' Mum wielded her own shears dramatically. 'What kind of haircut shall we give this tree today? A mohawk? Short back and sides? A nineteen-twenties bob?'

Alex snorted a laugh. 'Seriously?'

Mum nodded, her face earnest. 'That's the rule Mamma set. You have to decide the style before you start.'

'Okay then …' Alex pondered the question. 'A mullet. Party at the back, business at the front.'

Mum grinned. 'An excellent choice, daughter of mine.'

Talking and laughing with Mum as they snipped branches in the warm sunshine actually made the world start to feel vaguely normal again, and for a while Alex forgot about all the weirdness of the morning.

But that feeling didn't last long.

As she was working on the trees near the perimeter of the paddock, she heard a throat being cleared. She turned. The chocolate-coloured alpaca was leaning over the fence, the others huddled just behind. Alex quickly averted her eyes, focusing very hard on the branch in front of her. *Go away, go away, go away*, she willed silently.

'Hurry up and ask her,' a male voice said.

A different, deeper male voice answered. 'Be patient. We mustn't rush this.'

Alex glanced at Mum, to see if she could hear the voices

too. But Mum was oblivious to the conversation that was happening between the animals. *The conversation you imagine is happening,* Alex corrected herself. *Because this can't be real.*

'Excuse me.' It was the same female voice that Alex had run away from earlier. 'I don't mean to interrupt your gardening but … are you able to understand us?'

Alex's pulse quickened. This sounded way too real to be just happening in her imagination. Maybe she was going slowly crazy? Or perhaps there was some kind of growth on her brain that made her think she could hear animals talk? But what if it didn't stop with the alpacas and she started to hear other things? She'd already heard the wind speak to her when she arrived. That had sounded different to these current voices. What was going to be next? A fence post? A door? Her *sneakers*?

The chocolate alpaca tried again, leaning further over the fence. 'We just want to talk to you about …' She cast a furtive glance around and lowered her voice slightly. 'About you know what.'

Alex did not know what, and did not *want* to know what.

'Oh look,' Mum said, glancing up. 'The alpacas have come to say hello.'

'We should get away from them,' Alex said. 'Grandpa Jacob said they, um, bite. Really badly.'

'We don't bite.' The chocolate alpaca sounded wounded. She turned to the others. 'We'd never hurt anyone, would we?'

The other alpacas all answered at the same time.

'As if!'

'Wouldn't dream of it.'

'Not unless they deserved it.'

Mum laughed. 'They sound so funny, don't they? Like they're trying to hum a song.'

'Hum a song!' The male black alpaca said indignantly. 'We absolutely do not sound like that.'

The caramel alpaca shrugged. 'Apparently that's *exactly* what we sound like to humans.'

'Mum, I really, really think we should leave them alone.' Alex's voice now had an edge of panic to it.

Mum moved slowly toward the fence. She held out her hand and then started to stroke the neck of the black animal. 'They're okay,' Mum said, laughing as the animal closed his eyes and nuzzled into Mum's hand.

'A little to the left,' he muttered, 'a little more … oh yeah, that's the spot.'

'They're so tame,' Mum said. 'Didn't Dad say they just turned up here nine or ten years ago? I wonder where from.'

The black alpaca snorted. 'Lady, we've been here a bit longer than ten years. Times that by …' he trailed off and looked at the caramel-coloured one.

'Ninety-nine,' she said without missing a beat.

Maths wasn't Alex's strongest subject but even she knew that this came to nearly a thousand. Was this alpaca seriously trying to say that they had been here for a *thousand years*?

The talking was bad enough, but that was … preposterous!

'I'm going inside.' She didn't wait for Mum to answer before she took off at a run towards the farmhouse. She hadn't even made it outside the grove before the back door swung open and Grandpa Jacob came barrelling down the path as fast as his fractured foot would allow. Alex stopped in her tracks. What was worse? Her foul-tempered grandfather, or talking alpacas?

'Hey!' he shouted at Mum. 'What the devil do you think you're doing in there?'

'Just tidying up the trees,' Mum said.

Grandpa Jacob was shaking. 'No one touches those trees except Rosa!'

'They need a bit of a prune, Dad,' Mum said. 'They'll fruit better this way.'

'Get away from them!' he shouted.

'I'm just trying to help,' Mum said.

'Why won't you listen to me!' Grandpa Jacob bellowed, snatching the shears from her hands. 'I don't need your help!'

A muscle ticked in Mum's jaw. The alpacas slipped away. Birds flitted noisily from tree to tree as the softest of breezes caressed the tips of the olive grove.

Alex waited for the explosion, for Mum to start yelling, but it didn't come. When Mum eventually spoke, her voice was even and calm, and just a bit higher than normal. 'There's barely any food in the house. I'm going to go and buy some groceries for dinner.'

'I'll come with you,' Alex said quickly.

Mum didn't look Alex in the eye. 'That's okay, sweetheart. I think I'll go on my own.'

Alex opened her mouth to protest, but the rumble of an engine made them all turn. A red truck had pulled through the gate and was driving up towards the house.

# Chapter Five

The truck came to a stop next to the olive grove. When the driver's door swung open, Alex did a double-take. The boy who scrambled out was smaller than most of the kids in her class, all limbs and freckles, swimming inside clothes a few sizes too big. The only thing that fit properly was a scuffed brown drover's hat, which he had pulled down low on his head. Alex would have bet her favourite hoodie that he was nowhere near old enough to have his driver's licence.

He caught sight of Alex and her mum and promptly removed his hat. An avalanche of sandy brown hair flopped across eyes of roughly the same colour. Without the hat, he looked even younger. Alex stared at him, wary, adding this truck-driving kid to the growing list of things-too-weird-to-try-and-explain that she'd seen today.

'You were supposed to be here an hour ago,' Grandpa Jacob said. His words were curt, but all the sting in his voice from before was gone. He sounded almost … friendly?

'Sorry, Mr Ortiz,' the boy said. 'Deliveries are a bit

delayed this morning.' He looked back to Alex and Mum, confusion etched over his face. 'Didn't you say Wilfred was coming?'

'He will be,' Grandpa Jacob said stubbornly. 'Just as soon as I can get a hold of his father.'

Mum didn't bother to hide her eye roll. 'They're in Europe for a holiday. I'm Elina, Mr Ortiz's daughter. And this is Alex, his granddaughter. We're here instead.'

'I'm Leeuwin Bremmer,' he said. 'But everyone calls me Leeuie.'

'Bremmer?' Mum frowned. 'You're on the farm a few miles over? Apples?'

'Yes Ma'am. Largest apple orchard in the southern hemisphere.'

'And you, er, drove here?' Her eyes darted to the red truck. 'By yourself?'

He gave her a strange look, as though she had asked him if water was wet, or the sun was hot. 'Yes, Ma'am.'

'You're not … a bit young?'

He tried to stand a little taller. 'I'll be twelve in April.'

'I thought you had to be seventeen to get your licence,' Mum said, in that tone of voice that sounded like a question but wasn't.

'You do,' Leeuie said, 'but no one cares as long as you don't go on the highway.'

Mum arched an eyebrow in total disagreement, but didn't say anything. Grandpa Jacob wasn't paying any attention to the conversation and had instead unlatched the back of the truck and was trying to heave one of the boxes towards him. He wobbled precariously on his fractured foot. Leeuie and Mum rushed over to him at the same time.

'Stop your fussing,' he said, brushing Mum away.

Leeuie took the box gently from his hands. 'Let me help with that, Mr Ortiz.'

Grandpa Jacob considered this and nodded. 'Okay, thank you, Leeuie.'

And then he turned and stomped back inside without so much as a glance at Alex and Mum.

Alex stared. Did her grandfather just say *thank you*? He couldn't be bothered to say a single nice thing to his own daughter or granddaughter, or even remember Alex's name for that matter, but some random kid turns up and he becomes all smiles and sunshine. She reformulated her observation from earlier. It wasn't people in general Grandpa Jacob was horrible to. It was just her and Mum.

Mum peered into the back of the truck where more wooden crates were stacked. 'Are all of those for Dad?'

Leeuie nodded. 'For his alpacas. Apples are their favourite.'

At the mention of the alpacas, Alex's ears pricked up. She scrutinised Leeuie to see if there were any telltale signs he knew these were not ordinary alpacas. But he gave nothing away.

'I should get to the shops,' Mum said. 'Maybe you could

help Leeuie unload those apples and he can fill you in on what there is to do around here?'

Leeuie's face lit up at this idea. But Alex already knew what there was to do around here. Avoid talking alpacas, freaky winds and cranky grandfathers. She looked imploringly at Mum. 'Can't I come with you?'

Mum hesitated. 'I won't be gone long,' she said, and Alex could tell from her tone that she really wanted some alone time. 'You'll be okay.'

Alex nodded miserably and tried to convince herself that Mum was right.

# CHAPTER SIX

Leeuie unclipped a trolley from the back of the truck. 'Are you staying for the whole summer?' he asked, hopefully, passing down one of the boxes for Alex to load on the trolley.

The box was heavier than Alex expected and she grimaced. Up until this morning she had been thrilled by the prospect of a whole summer on the farm. It was something different, exciting. But she did not sign up for the kind of different or exciting that this place offered! Now, the thought of her familiar apartment — devoid of all animals, talking or not — was intoxicating. 'Not sure,' Alex said. 'I don't think so.' That last part was wishful thinking. She still had to convince Mum.

'Oh.' Leeuie tried to hide his disappointment. 'There's heaps of stuff to do, but not many people visit out here. Your cousin comes every year but … he's never interested in doing much.'

Alex accepted another box from Leeuie and stacked it

on the trolley. 'Don't you have friends from school that live around here?'

'I do distance ed,' he said. 'It's all online.'

'Your parents?'

'They're really busy with the farm. We have the biggest apple orchard in the southern hemisphere.'

'Yeah,' Alex said, 'you already mentioned that.'

Leeuie didn't clock her sarcasm and sighed, wistfully. 'I can't wait until next year when I go to boarding school. Then I'll have tonnes of friends around all the time.'

Alex didn't have the heart to tell Leeuie that this wasn't exactly how friendships worked. He heaved another box over the side of the truck to her. This was the heaviest one yet, and it slipped from her grasp and thumped heavily onto the other boxes.

'Ow!' Alex cried. A painful throb burned through her thumb where a splinter from the box had lodged itself under her thumbnail. Involuntary tears of pain filled her eyes and she shook her hand hard. How was it she'd managed to go her whole life without getting any splinters, but a single morning on a farm and she'd got two in as many hours?

Leeuie peered at it. 'That's nasty. But don't worry, I can get it out.' He unclipped a hunting knife from his belt and removed its leather sheath. The blade glinted grey and sharp.

'Uh, I'm fine. I can barely feel it,' Alex lied, keeping her eyes on the giant knife. What was a kid her age doing walking around with something like that?

'It could get infected.'

'I said it's fine!'

'It won't hurt. I've had lots of practice.' He showed
her his palms, which were streaked with faint white scars.
'Although,' he added wistfully, 'Dad says I need a few more
before I'm ready to run the farm.'

Alex couldn't care less about Leeuie's dad's position on
the number of splinters required for farm-running, because
her thumb was now pulsing with white-hot pain.

'I promise it won't hurt,' Leeuie repeated.

She glanced towards the house. The door was still firmly
shut. It was unlikely that Grandpa Jacob could be counted
on for first-aid support.

Alex reluctantly held out her hand. She felt the lightest
pressure and then a quick flick. Leeuie returned the knife to
its sheath and clipped it back on his belt.

Alex inspected her thumb. Blood pooled beneath the
nail, but Leeuie had been right: it hadn't hurt at all. She
shoved her thumb in her mouth to suck the blood off, then
immediately made a face and spat onto the ground. Gross!
Her thumb tasted like it had pruned olive trees, been covered
in alpaca spit and carried crates of apples. So, basically totally
disgusting.

Just then, an ear-splitting primal shriek came from high
above her. Her thumb forgotten, Alex yelped, cowering
beneath her arms.

Leeuie burst out laughing. 'Sorry,' he said, and he really did sound sorry. 'But it's just a bird.'

Alex glowered at Leeuie. Maybe if he wanted friends, he shouldn't laugh at people after they had just got a splinter and then a shock in quick succession. She shaded her eyes against the sun and looked up to where a huge bird circled above the farm, its white feathers dazzling in the sun. Saying this was 'just a bird' was like saying Mount Everest was just a hill. The creature's wingspan would have been as long as Alex's bed at home, and its talons could probably pierce a metal roof.

'I guess she could be a bit intimidating if you haven't seen her before,' Leeuie added. 'She's a white-bellied sea eagle, proper binomial nomenclature *Haliaeetus leucogaster*. She lives in the forest, which I know sounds weird because she's a sea eagle, but they can build their nests up to a thousand kilometres inland,' he added, as though Alex had asked or even cared.

The eagle completed another circle above them, screeching again. 'Why does it keep doing that?' Alex asked.

Leeuie frowned. 'I don't know. I've never seen her this close to the farm before.'

The eagle let out one final cry and then turned course sharply, back towards the forest. Leeuie watched the bird disappear between the trees. 'Dad says the family of them have been here forever. I was planning to hike out to the forest this summer and study her nesting behaviour as part of a science project. I think I've figured out the coordinates of the nest and …' He trailed off, his face scrunching up in confusion.

Alex followed his gaze. Huge storm clouds had gathered above the middle of the forest, thick and swirling, like some kind of other-worldly vortex. Alex's stomach flipped. 'Um, what is that?'

'A summer storm?' Leeuie said, but he sounded far from certain.

The billowy slate-grey mass condensed and grew, shifting and changing like a living organism. Alex's skin prickled. A tiny fragment of a thought started to take shape in her mind. The wind that had come from the forest earlier had started when she touched the symbol on the wooden post. And now this crazy mess of clouds was moving and swirling above the forest. Was the symbol somehow connected to this, too?

'Leeuie,' she said urgently, 'do you know anything about the symbols carved into the fences?'

'Sort of,' Leeuie said absently, still staring at the sky. 'I mean, I know they're something to do with your family history and the reason Mr Ortiz lives here. How come?'

Alex didn't know exactly. She couldn't quite make sense of anything yet.

Within moments, the clouds blanketed the whole forest, giving the afternoon a horribly apocalyptic kind of feel. Then the wind started. Light at first, but quickly becoming stronger, racing through the olive trees and hurtling twigs and leaves through the air.

Suddenly, a fork of lightning emerged from the centre of the forest and spiked upwards, striking the clouds, electrifying them with blue and green and purple.

Alex jumped, skin tingling, pulse racing. Lightning wasn't supposed to do that, was it?

'Did you see that!' Leeuie cried.

Before Alex could respond the clouds started to race across the sky, towards the farmhouse, faster and faster. They were sparking and tingling with electrified energy.

Grandpa Jacob appeared at the back door. 'Get in the house!' His voice was almost carried away by the wind. 'Hurry!'

Within seconds, the clouds were directly above them, a writhing mass that blocked out the sun and plunged the whole farm into inky darkness. The wind screamed like a train about to go off its rails. Leaves and sticks and dirt shot in every direction. Overhead, thunder curdled and roared.

'Come on!' Leeuie cried, and he took off, vanishing into the darkness.

'Leeuie?' Alex squinted into the gloom. She was all turned around. 'Leeuie!' She looked back and forth, trying to figure out which way he'd gone. Which way the house was.

A shard of lightning ripped through the air and slammed into the ground metres from where she stood. The earth exploded. Alex screamed.

'Alex?' Leeuie's voice sounded tiny and very far away. 'Alex? Where are you?'

'I'm here!' Alex screamed, although she didn't even really know where here was. And then she started to run.

# CHAPTER SEVEN

Alex had only gone a few steps when she slammed into something. A fence! The olive grove! Her heart pounded as she scrambled over the wooden railing. She pushed through the trees, heading deeper in the grove. In the dark, she stumbled into roots and bashed against branches.

There was another tremendous pop. The sky flared white. The olive tree next to her ignited in a deafening whoosh. A wall of searing heat blasted Alex. She jumped back, heart hammering. From above, lightning pierced through the clouds, striking tree after tree after tree. Scorching heat radiated outward as flames licked furiously at the sky.

Alex cried out in panic. She had to get out of here. Now!

She tried to run, but within seconds the smoke engulfed her. Her eyes streamed, vision blurry from soot and tears. Every breath she took was suffocating. The heat from the flames surrounding her was so intense she felt like her skin might melt right off. She choked down a sob, turning this way and that, trying to see a path. But there was nothing except fire all around.

No place to run.

No one to help.

Nothing but flames and fumes and total destruction.

And then, somehow, amongst it all, Alex had a single, perfect moment of clarity. She was not going to die. Not like this. Not today. Not before Mum got home from the shops. Not before her grandfather learned her name. And not before she figured out what *on earth* was going on here.

Alex covered her mouth with the sleeve of her hoodie and barrelled forward. And then suddenly, through the haze and smoke, there was the grove fence. And there were Grandpa Jacob and Leeuie! With a movement that could only be described as a headfirst tumble, Alex launched herself up and over the fence.

Leeuie grabbed at her arm. 'We've gotta get out of here!'

Grandpa Jacob was staring at the burning trees, his mouth slack. The light from the flames made dancing orange patterns across his face.

'Grandpa Jacob,' Alex croaked. 'We really need to go.'

The flames devoured the last of the olive trees, careening toward them like a fiery wave. But still Grandpa Jacob did not move.

Alex thought they were done. The whole farm was about to be engulfed by the fire.

But then the flames stopped advancing — no, more than

that — they shrunk. The blaze sank lower and lower, like someone was turning off a gas stove. Within seconds, the noxious smoke vanished into the leaden sky overhead. The clouds hung above the farm for a few more seconds then vanished, taking the suffocating fumes with them. The late afternoon sun filled the valley once more.

For the longest time, none of them said anything. And then Leeuie spoke. 'Did that … did that just happen?'

Alex rubbed her swollen eyes, squinting against the painfully bright daylight. Her head felt too crowded, jammed with unanswered questions. She looked searchingly at Grandpa Jacob.

His expression was hollow and raw as he stared out over where the grove had been.

Alex frowned. She touched his arm, gently. 'Hey, Grandpa Jacob? Are you okay?'

'Rosa's trees …' His voice cracked and tears sprang to his eyes. 'They're all gone.'

# CHAPTER EIGHT

In the kitchen, Alex gulped down glassfuls of water. Grandpa Jacob sat heavily at the kitchen table, his eyes unfocused and red-rimmed, while Leeuie hovered nearby, unable to stand still.

'What *was* that?' Alex asked, when her throat felt normal again.

If Grandpa Jacob heard her he showed no signs of it.

Leeuie cleared his throat. 'I think it was a … freak electrical storm. I saw this show on the Discovery Channel about them. I'm sure that's what it was. Right, Mr Ortiz?' Leeuie sounded very far from sure.

'That was *not* an electrical storm,' Alex said.

'What else could it have been?' asked Leeuie.

They both looked at Grandpa Jacob. Still, he said nothing. Did nothing. It was like they weren't even there.

Alex's body felt like it was filled with cement. Maybe it *had* been a freak electrical storm. Maybe it hadn't. Maybe she didn't care either way anymore. All she wanted right now was to get clean.

'Where are you going?' Leeuie sounded panicked.

'Shower,' Alex said.

'Oh. Okay. I'll stay here and …' He looked around the kitchen, his eyes falling on the kettle. 'Tea! I'll make tea! My gran says that tea fixes everything.'

Alex personally favoured chocolate chip ice-cream as the solution to every problem, but Grandpa Jacob didn't seem like an ice-cream kind of guy. Besides, nothing was going to un-burn the olive grove.

In the bathroom, Alex stood under the scalding shower until the water ran clear. Finding her suitcase propped in the hallway, she put on fresh clothes and shoes, then pulled her hair into a ponytail. She felt human again. And it was time for answers.

Alex marched back into the kitchen. Grandpa Jacob had an untouched mug of steaming tea in front of him. She sat in the chair opposite. 'Tell me what started the fire.'

Still nothing. Frustrated, Alex pushed the tea towards him. He wrapped his big hands around the mug and took a long sip, closing his eyes for a brief moment.

'The fire,' Alex repeated, louder this time. 'What started it?'

Leeuie's gran must have been right about the restorative properties of tea, because all of a sudden Grandpa Jacob was back.

He pushed himself to standing. 'Leeuie, tell your dad I'll settle the account for the apples another day.' He spoke as though nothing out of the ordinary had happened at all. As if this were a perfectly normal farm, and today was a perfectly normal day. 'You can show yourselves out. I have things to do.'

And then he thumped his way across the kitchen and into a narrow passageway next to the fridge. Alex balled her fists in exasperation. She knew there was something weird going on, Leeuie knew there was something weird going on, Grandpa Jacob definitely knew there was something weird going on, so why wouldn't he just tell her what it was?

She scrambled up and followed him through the passage. It was a walk-in pantry, each shelf organised neatly with stacks of bottles, jars and tins. At the end of the passage was a wooden door, which Grandpa Jacob disappeared through, slamming it behind him. There was a metallic clunk as a key turned in a lock.

Alex glowered at the door.

'I think he wants to be left alone,' Leeuie said.

Alex didn't care what he wanted. He owed her answers. And she was going to get them.

# CHAPTER NINE

Alex banged on the door, not stopping until the key turned again and Grandpa Jacob's irate face appeared.

'I'm busy,' he snapped.

Alex slipped under his arm before he had a chance to stop her. The room was cosy, each wall lined with brimming bookshelves. In the middle of the room was a wooden desk covered in stacks of papers. At the back of the room, a window overlooked the burnt olive grove.

'Tell me what did that!' Alex demanded, pointing out the window.

'It's none of your concern!'

'Tell me!'

Grandpa Jacob raised his voice to match hers. 'I will not be ordered around in my own house! Get out!'

'Not until you tell me what just happened!'

He glared at her. 'It's none of your —'

Alex's rage boiled then overflowed. 'It *is* my concern! I nearly *died*!'

That brought Grandpa Jacob up short.

Hovering in the door, Leeuie looked anxiously from Alex to Grandpa Jacob.

Alex took a breath. 'Tell me what's going on,' she said, calmer. 'Maybe I can help?'

Grandpa Jacob shook his head. 'You can't.'

'How do you know?'

'Because I do.'

Alex swallowed down a groan. Mum had been right about him being as stubborn as a goat. 'You can't possibly know if I can help or not. You don't know anything about me.'

'I know enough to know you can't help,' he shot back.

'But —'

Grandpa Jacob had had enough. 'How many times do I need to tell you!' he bellowed. 'You can't help!' He stamped his fractured leg on the ground so hard that the books on the shelves jumped. All the blood rushed from his face and a string of expletives flew out of his mouth. He sank into a chair, clutching his leg, still cursing.

*Serves you right*, Alex thought, but then immediately felt guilty. 'Do you need help?'

'No!' Grandpa Jacob shouted. 'I. Do. Not. Need. Help!' He squeezed his eyes shut, grimacing. 'There's tablets in the kitchen. Yellow bottle.'

Alex hesitated. 'You want me to get them for you?'

'No, I want you to stand there gaping like a goldfish!'

Alex wanted to let him wallow in the pain of his broken foot but, given the sheet-white colour of his face, decided against it. She brushed past Leeuie and raced through the pantry into the kitchen. On the counter were two yellow pill bottles with identical pharmacy labels. She took both to the study.

Grandpa Jacob waved away the bottle in her left hand. 'Those make me fall asleep. Horrid things.' He took the other bottle, tipping out a pill and swallowing it without water. He stared into space for a few moments then slumped back into the chair.

'Are you okay, Mr Ortiz?' Leeuie said, still in the doorway.

For a few moments the old man said nothing. And then he let out a heavy sigh. 'I just don't know what to do,' he muttered, more to himself than his audience. 'It's begun and I don't know how to stop it.'

'*What's* begun?' Alex couldn't keep the frustration out of her voice. 'How to stop *what*?'

He put his head in his hands and said nothing.

Alex glared at him. Well, okay, fine. If he wasn't going to tell her, she would just start guessing and not stop until he spilled the beans. And she had a pretty good idea where to start. The strange symbol. The one Leeuie said was something to do with their family history. The one Grandpa Jacob had refused to tell her about.

'The symbol made the fire start, didn't it.' Alex spoke

with the same certainty Mum used when she knew Alex was not being totally truthful about something. Like when Alex claimed she truly had no idea what happened to the packet of chocolate biscuits and maybe Mum accidentally left it at the store?

Grandpa Jacob jerked his head up. 'What do you know about that symbol?'

*Bingo,* Alex thought. She repeated what Leeuie had told her earlier. 'It represents our family history and it's the reason you live here.' She paused. 'And it's connected to something in the forest. Something that started the fire.' Leeuie hadn't told her that bit, but Alex was sure she was right.

Grandpa Jacob scrutinised her. Alex stared back at him, not blinking. He looked away first. His eyes brushed over Leeuie, but the boy had obviously passed whatever test Grandpa Jacob deemed necessary for hearing this big secret.

'Alright,' he said. 'Seeing as you're so eager to know, I'll tell you.'

Alex sucked in a breath. Finally!

Grandpa Jacob stared at the ceiling for a frustratingly long time. 'This is not an ordinary farm,' he eventually said in a low, secretive voice.

Alex rolled her eyes. Seriously? It didn't take a genius to figure *that* one out.

Grandpa Jacob continued. 'The land belonged to my father. And before that my father's father, and before that my fa—'

'I get it,' Alex said, 'it's been in the family for ages.'

He regarded her coolly. 'If you're going to constantly interrupt, this will take quite some time.'

'I interrupted once!'

'That's twice now,' he said.

Alex made a show of pretending to zip up her mouth and lock it.

'My point,' Grandpa Jacob said with a stern look, 'is that I am not here by accident. My family bought this land several generations ago because it is our duty to protect it.'

Alex forgot about her locked mouth. 'Protect it from what?'

'Not from what. From whom,' Grandpa Jacob said. He lowered his voice. 'From Kiala.'

Alex hesitated. Was that name supposed to mean something to her? She looked to Leeuie, to see if the name registered with him, but he looked as confused as she did.

'Who's Kiala?' she asked.

'Shhhh!' Grandpa Jacob winced, glancing to the open window. 'Kiala is a powerful spirit who is imprisoned in the forest here.'

If Alex hadn't already been subjected to eerie winds, freak firestorms and talking animals, she would have started laughing. But after those, a spirit in a forest seemed scarily credible. Still … 'Why is a spirit imprisoned in the forest here?'

'Because …' Grandpa Jacob trailed off, then sighed. 'I suppose I may as well start from the start.'

# Chapter Ten

'Many thousands of years ago, there was a wandering tribe of people called the Chodzanar. They had a special gift that no other living beings had: the ability to harness nature's power and channel it into other living forms. They travelled around the globe helping villages and towns ravaged by disaster. They could restore balance to crop cycles or livestock breeding patterns by stabilising the two dimensions of nature's power.'

Alex frowned. She was already confused. 'What do you mean by the two dimensions of nature's power?'

'Regeneration and destruction.' He said this in a way that indicated he thought anyone who didn't know it was an idiot.

'Destruction?' Alex said, ignoring his tone. 'Like hurricanes and bushfires and stuff?'

'That's correct.'

'Why would you want to channel destruction into anything?'

From his position in the doorway, Leeuie chimed in. 'Actually, destruction's important because without it, you can't have regeneration. You have to clear out the old to make way for the new. I saw this program on the Discovery Channel about it. Did you know that eucalyptus trees only realise it's time to regenerate when they smell the smoke from a bushfire? If there was no fire — no destruction — they'd never be able to regenerate. It's about having a balance.'

Grandpa Jacob nodded, then looked at Alex. 'Can I go on with the story now?'

'Yeah,' Alex mumbled, scowling in Leeuie's direction. *Know-it-all.*

'One day the tribe stumbled across a small mountainous village high in the Andes that had been devastated by a series of disasters. All of the villagers had perished or fled. All except a young woman who was heavily pregnant. She was on the brink of death herself and begged the Chodzanar to channel their gift into her child, to give it a chance of survival.'

Leeuie's eyes widened. 'Did they do it?'

'Yes. But when the woman gave birth, there was not one child, but two. Identical twin girls, called Kiala and Resila. And the gift had been split between them. Resila could control nature's regenerative forces and Kiala could control nature's forces of destruction.'

'That is so awesome,' Leeuie said.

'The mother didn't survive much longer,' Grandpa

Jacob continued, 'so the Chodzanar tribe adopted the babies and raised them as their own. By the time the girls were twelve years old, they were incredibly powerful. Kiala could summon a storm to flatten a crop in three seconds flat, and Resila could command the crop to regrow just as fast.'

'So, Kiala lives here now?' Alex asked. 'And if she's here, where's the sister?'

Grandpa Jacob gave her a sharp look for interrupting again. 'Despite their immense powers, the girls were only human. And, like any other siblings, wanted different things from their lives. While Resila was content traveling around with the Chodzanar and helping those in need, Kiala wanted more. She'd had a taste for what great power felt like and didn't want to let go. She tried to convince her sister to leave with her. "We will take over the world," she said. "We will make everyone kneel before us. They will treat us like gods." But Resila knew no good would come of that, so she told the Chodzanar of her sister's plan.'

Leeuie was the one who interrupted this time. 'Did they manage to stop her in time?'

Grandpa Jacob shook his head sadly. 'Kiala was too strong. Too angry. She sent earthquakes and storms, forest fires and hurricanes. She managed to wipe out most of the Chodzanar tribe in a matter of minutes. Then she destroyed her sister.'

Alex's breath caught in her throat. 'Kiala *killed* her own sister?'

Grandpa Jacob nodded gravely. 'Kiala knew that her twin sister's power was the only magic strong enough to kill her. And so she got in first.'

Alex cast a glance over the destroyed olive grove and shuddered.

Grandpa Jacob continued. 'The only people who survived were the four strongest Chodzanar warriors. They devised a plan to stop Kiala. They weren't powerful enough to kill her, but they found a way to imprison her. They performed a complicated ritual that separated Kiala's body from her spirit, then trapped the spirit in an enchanted prison and hid her deep in the forest here, as far from her home as possible. The magic that binds her lasts a thousand years. After that, the spell has to be performed again.'

Alex gulped. 'So a thousand years is up?'

'No.' Grandpa Jacob raked a hand through his hair. 'That's what I don't understand. We're supposed to have another ten years.'

Now it was Leeuie's turn to look stricken. 'Then how has she escaped?'

'She hasn't escaped,' Grandpa Jacob explained. 'We wouldn't be sitting here if that was the case. But she's woken up. Somehow, she's woken up.'

Alex went rigid. When she had arrived at the farm, she had touched the symbol by the fence post, and the gust of wind — which she was now positive was Kiala's doing — had whooshed out of the forest and whispered in her ear. She almost didn't dare ask, but she had to know.

'Those symbols on the fence posts,' she said, very casually, 'they're not, like, buttons or something, are they?'

Grandpa Jacob frowned. 'Buttons?'

'Say someone accidentally pressed one. Would it wake her up?'

'Of course not!' Grandpa Jacob snorted.

Alex puffed out a relieved breath. At least it wasn't her fault that Kiala was awake.

'I have no idea what's roused her after all this time,' Grandpa Jacob continued. 'But from here, she'll only get stronger, and her prison weaker. It's only a matter of time before …' He shuddered, unable to even say the words.

But he didn't need to say it out loud. Alex got it, loud and clear. Kiala escapes, everything dies.

'You know how to perform the ritual, don't you?' Alex said. 'To make her prison strong again?'

'Not personally,' Grandpa Jacob said. 'But there is a prophecy that tells us who does.'

'A prophecy?' Alex repeated. Didn't prophecies only happen in books and movies?

Grandpa Jacob regarded her coolly. 'Do you have a problem with prophecies?'

Alex hesitated. Ordinarily, yes. But today had been anything but ordinary. 'No.'

'Then may I continue without you interrupting me again?' Grandpa Jacob asked. Without waiting for an answer, he rifled through a sturdy black bowl on his desk, which was filled with keys of various shapes and sizes. He found the one he was looking for and slotted it into the lock of his desk drawer. He took out a thick, leather-bound journal, worn and yellowed with age. It was filled with pages and pages of handwritten scrawl. He flipped to a page, and read aloud.

*'The power returns with the Fortieth Son,*
*it's thanks to their blood that the task can be done.*
*The Son has the gift,*
*the Guardians, lore*
*to rebind the spirit before there is war.'*

He closed the journal again and rested it on his desk, letting the words hang in the air.

Alex blinked a few times, trying to make sense of what he'd just said. She could only come to one conclusion: if that poem was meant to tell them how to stop Kiala then they were even more stuffed than she'd originally thought.

# Chapter Eleven

Alex said as much to Grandpa Jacob, and he frowned at her over the top of his glasses.

'I didn't say it was an instruction manual,' he grumbled. 'But it does tell us what needs to happen next.'

Alex couldn't disagree more. One thing that prophecy was *not* was a clear outline for what to do when you've got a destructive spirit trying to escape from a magical prison.

Leeuie leaned over Grandpa Jacob's shoulder, moving his lips silently as he recited the poem to himself over and over. He was looking equally confused, and Alex felt a sliver of satisfaction that she wasn't the only one stumped.

'Hmmm,' Leeuie eventually said. '*The power returns with the Fortieth Son, it's thanks to their blood that the task can be done.*' He looked to Grandpa Jacob. 'The Fortieth Son is a person? And it's something about his blood that stops Kiala? Is that the gift that it talks about?' He pointed to the third line, *The Son has the gift.*

'Very close!' Grandpa Jacob gave Leeuie an approving

gaze. Leeuie flushed with happiness. Alex's sliver of
satisfaction melted into annoyance.

'The Fortieth Son is indeed a person,' Grandpa Jacob
explained. 'But it's not his blood exactly that will stop Kiala.
Rather, this is talking about the fact he's the fortieth son in a
particular bloodline.'

Alex frowned. She looked over the prophecy again.
'Where does it say that?'

'It doesn't,' Grandpa Jacob said, impatiently. 'But it's
my job, as Guardian, to know the real meaning behind the
prophecy. And we find this Fortieth Son' — he tapped the
page in the journal — 'by counting the eldest son in each
generation. You understand?'

Alex's head hurt from trying to understand. But she
didn't say so.

'Whose bloodline is it?' Leeuie asked.

'Mine,' Grandpa Jacob said. 'I'm descended from one of
the warriors who originally captured Kiala's spirit.'

'You're descended from a warrior?' Leeuie was awestruck.
'That is the coolest thing ever.'

'Um, hello, so am I,' Alex said.

Grandpa Jacob looked surprised. 'Yes, I suppose you are.
Sort of.'

Alex glowered. There was no sort of about it. She was
related to Grandpa Jacob, so she was related to the warrior.

Grandpa Jacob continued. 'This warrior possessed a
special kind of power, which was then dormant for thirty-

nine generations. But with the birth of the Fortieth Son — the eldest son in the fortieth generation — the power returns. This man is the only person who has the ability to stop Kiala.'

Leeuie nodded. 'Okay, so the Fortieth Son has the gift, which is the power to stop Kiala. And it says the Guardians have lore.' He turned to Alex. 'That means wisdom.'

'I know,' Alex said. Well, she did now at least.

'So the Fortieth Son and the Guardians are meant to team up and stop Kiala, otherwise she'll start killing everyone again,' he finished.

'That's correct,' Grandpa Jacob said.

'Are you the Fortieth Son?' Leeuie asked cautiously, trying to hide the fact he didn't fancy the chances of an old man with a fractured foot against a spirit of destruction.

'No, no, not me,' Grandpa Jacob said. 'I'm just the Guardian.'

Leeuie was relieved. 'Who is it?'

Alex groaned. Of course. 'Wilfred's the Fortieth Son, right?'

Grandpa Jacob nodded. 'And this summer I'd planned to tell him about his destiny so he would have a decade to train and prepare for the task ahead.'

Alex nodded slowly. So *that's* why Grandpa Jacob had been so set on Uncle Neil and Wilfred coming out for the summer.

'Does his dad know about this?' Leeuie asked.

Grandpa Jacob shook his head. 'Oh no. Neil is … well, let's just say he's always been a bit challenged in the imagination department. I'm not sure he would have believed me.'

Alex couldn't argue with that. Uncle Neil was even more into logic and common sense than Mum. His idea of a bedtime story was reciting the nine times table.

'Then why didn't you tell someone else?' Alex asked. *Like me.* 'In case something happened to you before you got a chance to fill Wilfred in on the details?'

'I wrote everything down.' Grandpa Jacob said, tapping the leather-bound book he'd taken out of the drawer. 'If something happened to me, this journal would have gone to Wilfred when he turned fourteen. It contains everything I know.'

'Why fourteen?' Leeuie asked. 'Why didn't you tell him when he was younger?'

'Because Kiala was supposed to be asleep for another ten years,' Grandpa Jacob said, exasperated. He was clearly getting sick of this line of questioning. 'Plus, my father told me about Kiala when I was fourteen. It's a good age. Not too young to be incompetent, not too old to be disbelieving.'

Leeuie looked a bit stung at the incompetent comment.

Alex, on the other hand, felt quite a bit better. Not because the whole fate of the world and everything in it rested on the shoulders of her computer game-obsessed cousin, but because it suddenly explained why Grandpa

Jacob was only interested in spending time with his grandson. It wasn't personal that he didn't want Alex or Mum around. It was fate. Or something. Now she just had to find a way to tell Mum that — preferably in a way that didn't involve any mention of ancient spirits or prophecies or firestorms …

But that was a problem for later. Right now, there were more pressing matters. Like the fact that Wilfred was in Europe with his parents and Alex couldn't see any situation (that didn't involve someone dying) in which they would willingly cut their trip short.

# Chapter Twelve

'What's going to happen if Wilfred doesn't come back in time?' Alex asked.

'That's not an option!' Grandpa Jacob stood up from his chair and started pacing the small room, his footsteps an uneven tread. *Step-thump, step-thump, step-thump.* 'I'll keep calling Neil,' he muttered. 'He has to listen to me. He has to bring Wilfred home.'

Leeuie watched the pacing too, fiddling with his hat. 'Is there something I can do to help in the meantime?' he ventured. 'I know I'm not the Fortieth Son, but I go into the forest quite a bit. I know my way around.'

'No,' Grandpa Jacob said. 'It's too dangerous.'

'But I could do some reconnaissance.'

Alex gave him an incredulous look. Of course Leeuie would offer to do something like wander into a forest where an evil spirit lived.

'Absolutely not.' Grandpa Jacob stopped walking and fixed his piercing dark eyes on the boy. 'Promise me you won't go in there.'

'Okay, I promise,' Leeuie said, but he didn't sound happy about it. 'But we need a plan.'

Grandpa Jacob resumed his pacing. 'I'm thinking, I'm thinking.'

Alex still couldn't wrap her head around the fact that her cousin was supposed to be the only person on the face of the earth who could stop an evil spirit from destroying the world. He just seemed so … unlikely. 'Is there any chance you made a mistake about who the Fortieth Son is?' Alex said.

Grandpa Jacob stopped pacing. 'What kind of mistake?'

'Maybe … it's not the eldest son in each generation? It could be, I don't know, the second or third son?'

Grandpa Jacob snorted. 'It's not.'

'Or … maybe you counted down the number of relatives wrong?'

'I did no such thing!'

'Are you sure?' Alex pressed.

'Positive.'

'*Positive* positive?'

He gave Alex a withering look.

'It couldn't hurt to triple-check,' Leeuie said, in what Alex thought was a totally sucky tone. 'We could count them once more?'

'Fine.' Grandpa Jacob did not like having his judgement questioned, but he did take out a large piece of folded paper, which was tucked into the same drawer as the journal, and spread it out on top of the messy desk. 'Suit yourselves.'

The page was an eye-boggling array of words, written in tiny, spidery letters and connected together with lines. Alex recognised it as a family tree, albeit the most complicated and longwinded family tree she had ever seen.

Right at the top was an intricate drawing. A circle that surrounded a chunky cross and four small triangles, one at the end of each arm.

'That's the picture from the fence post!' Alex said.

'It's called the Amarlysa,' Grandpa Jacob said. 'It was the symbol of the Chodzanar tribe.' He smoothed the creases from the paper then tapped his finger to a name written at the top. *Moraika Sola Uarcay*. 'This is the warrior I'm descended from.'

*And me*, Alex thought, sounding out the syllables of the name in her head. *Moraika Sola Uarcay*.

'Her name means heavenly daughter of the sun,' Grandpa Jacob explained. 'She was, apparently, the bravest and most heroic warrior of the lot.'

Below that, a complicated waterfall of names cascaded over the sheet of paper, each connected with a line to the one above. Alex read through the unfamiliar names. *Fila Sole ... Pahuac Timme Mait ... Kehener Solan Wehner ...* The names became more modern and familiar the closer she got to the bottom. *Alberto Guerrero ... Susan Beatrice Sol ... Mitchell Renbre ...* Right at the end were Uncle Neil and Wilfred.

Alex and Mum were not listed anywhere.

'The eldest sons are written in a different colour,' Grandpa Jacob said. 'So you can more easily follow the path of the bloodline.'

Alex peered closer. Sure enough, there was one name in each generation that was written in a slightly darker ink.

'Well?' Grandpa Jacob drummed his fingers on the table. 'Did I count correctly?'

The finger-drumming noise and Grandpa Jacob's self-satisfied tone got on Alex's nerves, so she counted the names very slowly, just to irritate him. But even after counting them twice more, she came to the same conclusion. Wilfred was the Fortieth Son.

'Is it possible the prophecy is wrong?' she said, more to be contrary than because she thought it was a possibility. 'Like, it's actually the fifteenth, or the thirty-third person?'

Grandpa Jacob threw his hands into the air. 'If the prophecy was translated incorrectly, then your guess is as good as mine as to who the Fortieth Son is!'

A tiny nugget of a thought formed in the back of Alex's mind. She turned her grandfather's words over in her head. *If the prophecy was translated incorrectly … If the prophecy was translated incorrectly …* 'Did you translate it?' she asked.

Grandpa Jacob shook his head. 'That happened well before my time.'

Alex mulled over this. 'What if there was a mistake when it was first written down in English?'

Leeuie's eyes lit up. 'You think some words got mixed up?'

Grandpa Jacob gave them a sceptical glance. 'Why are you trying so hard to prove it's not Wilfred?'

Alex and Leeuie shared a quick look. *Because if the fate of the world rests with Wilfred we're in real trouble.*

'It's possible though, isn't it?' Alex pressed. She looked over the prophecy again, scrutinising each syllable.

*The power returns with the Fortieth Son,*
*it's thanks to their blood that the task can be done.*
*The Son has the gift,*
*the Guardians, lore*
*to rebind the spirit before there is war.*

And then it hit her. She turned to her grandfather. 'You said Moraika's name means daughter of sun or something?'

'Heavenly daughter of the sun,' he corrected.

'And which part means sun?'

'Her middle name,' Grandpa Jacob said. 'Sola.'

'What if the word for S-O-N and S-U-N got mixed up,' Alex said, talking fast, 'and it's the fortieth person in the bloodline with sun in their name instead!'

Her heart beat a little bit faster as she scanned over the family tree. She'd taken French, Italian and Spanish at school. She had been useless at them all, but there was one thing she remembered: a lot of the words looked and sounded almost the same in all three languages. 'Look at all the names that have similar words in them,' she said. 'Sol, Solis, Sole, Soleil …'

Leeuie gasped. 'They all mean sun in different languages!'

Grandpa Jacob didn't even get a chance to react before Leeuie and Alex started poring over the family tree. They read through the names together, pointing out each time a word similar to Sola cropped up.

When they got to the bottom, Alex's face fell. 'My great-great-grandmother is the thirty-ninth person, but no one after her has a word that means sun in their name.'

And then she froze.

She remembered what Grandpa Jacob had said when Alex had followed him through the olive grove to feed the alpacas. *This Olive Grove belongs to Rosa Surya Ortiz.* Surya was her grandmother's maiden name. It meant sun.

Surya was also Alex's middle name.

Her heart hammering, Alex grabbed a pencil from the table and started to write on the family tree.

'What the devil are you doing?' Grandpa Jacob blustered, but Leeuie stopped him from snatching the pencil from Alex's hand.

Alex added two rectangular boxes to the bottom of the chart. In the first one she wrote Mum's name: Elina Susan Ortiz. In the second, below her mother's and connected by a fine line, she wrote her own name: Alexandra Surya Harris.

Grandpa Jacob looked up sharply. 'Surya? Your middle name is Surya?'

Leeuie looked from Alex to Grandpa Jacob. 'What does that mean?'

'Surya was my wife's maiden name,' Grandpa Jacob explained. He stared at Alex as though seeing her properly for the first time. 'Surya means sun.'

'But then …' Leeuie's mouth fell open. 'Then you're the Fortieth Sun.'

# CHAPTER THIRTEEN

Afternoon light streamed in through the window of Grandpa Jacob's study, bathing the whole room in a soft warmth. Outside, the air was alive with birds and insects. Inside, Alex was unable to move. Unable to breathe.

She was the Fortieth Sun?

Her mind was a messy jumble of thoughts and feelings. She was so important that there was a whole prophecy written about her — a prophecy that had been passed down through generations and generations. The very idea of her existed before she ever had.

But being the Fortieth Sun meant that she had to go up against an ancient spirit of destruction who had been stuck in a forest for a gazillion years. And there was no way — *no way* — Alex could do that.

She didn't have the first idea about how to find Kiala's spirit, let alone do any magic spell to trap it in a prison. And what about this special gift Alex was supposed to have? She couldn't think of a single thing that she did better than anyone else in the world. Unless you counted her knack for coming up with excuses as to why she hadn't done her homework, or eating an entire jar of peanut butter without being sick. She couldn't run particularly fast, or jump especially high. She wasn't a maths whizz or an artistic genius or a science nerd. She was average. Her report card always confirmed it.

Grandpa Jacob's short laugh cut through her thoughts. 'You? You're the person who's supposed to stop Kiala?'

Alex's head stopped buzzing. She folded her arms over her chest, glaring defiantly at her grandfather. 'And why couldn't it be me?'

'Because you're just a ...' Grandpa Jacob waved his hand around in front of Alex, indicating that she was a girl. Like she didn't already know.

Alex glared harder. 'So? Moraika the warrior was a girl, too.'

Grandpa Jacob at least had the good grace to shift uncomfortably in his chair. 'Well ... er ... I just thought the Fortieth Sun would be more ...'

Leeuie jumped in. 'Of course it could be you.' He sounded almost jealous. 'So, what's your plan? How are you going to stop Kiala?'

'I only just found out that I have to,' Alex said through gritted teeth, 'so I don't really know yet.'

'Well, you have the gift,' Leeuie said. He turned to Grandpa Jacob. 'And you said you're the Guardian, Mr Ortiz.

So you're going to help her. That's what the prophecy says, right?'

Grandpa Jacob nodded numbly. 'Er, yes. Indeed. Any information you need to help with the task I can provide.'

Alex paused. 'Like what?'

'Like …' Grandpa Jacob absently rubbed his fractured foot. 'Weather patterns, descriptions of Kiala's physical attributes, psychological theories about her current state of mind.'

Alex blinked. Physical attributes? Weather patterns? She didn't think any of that was going to come in especially handy.

'But, as the prophecy states,' he added, opening the journal again and tapping the words of the poem. 'With your gift and my wisdom, together we'll be able to stop her.'

Alex looked at the page. She groaned loudly. How had she not put this together earlier? '*The Sun has the gift, the Guardians, lore,*' she recited. 'It says Guardians. Plural. As in, there's more than one.'

'Well, there's only me,' Grandpa Jacob said, stubbornly.

Alex shook her head. 'You're not the Guardian.'

He regarded Alex very coolly. 'Excuse me?'

In all the drama of the olive grove burning down and learning about Kiala and the Fortieth Sun, she had temporarily forgotten about her seemingly impossible encounter earlier that day with the alpacas. But now everything made sense. The prophecy said there was more than one Guardian and that Alex had a gift that no one else did. 'It's the alpacas,' she said. 'They're the Guardians.'

Leeuie looked very confused. 'The *alpacas* are the Guardians?'

'Preposterous!' Grandpa Jacob barked. 'What on earth would make you think that?'

'Because …' Alex cleared her throat, more for dramatic effect than because she needed to. 'I can understand them.'

Leeuie and Grandpa Jacob stared at her. Then they spoke at the same time. 'You can *understand* them?'

Alex nodded. 'And they can understand me. We can speak to each other.'

'Speak to each other?' Leeuie repeated.

Alex wondered if Leeuie was going to do that with everything she said from now on.

'That's right,' Alex confirmed. 'And I overheard one of them saying they'd been here for about a thousand years.'

'Well I can tell you they haven't,' Grandpa Jacob snorted. 'They turned up ten years ago. Just wandered up to the house. Sort of like they belonged here …' He realised what he was saying and trailed off. Blinked. Stared at Alex. 'You say they can *talk*?'

Alex nodded.

Grandpa Jacob stared at the ceiling, taking all this new information in. 'There were rumours,' he said slowly, 'that the four surviving Chodzanar warriors used the last of their powers to make themselves immortal. To separate their spirits from their bodies, like they did with Kiala, so they could inhabit new forms and watch over her. But I always assumed that was poppycock.' He shook his head, dumbfounded. 'I suppose I was wrong about that, too. The alpacas must be those warriors.'

The three of them looked out the study window. The alpacas were crowded together in the paddock, like four funny shaped balls of wool stuck onto slightly turned-out legs. They looked absolutely nothing like the ferocious warriors Alex had pictured in her head. But if it were true, then did that mean she was *related* to an alpaca? She shook her head slightly. Could this day get any weirder?

'I would have chosen to turn into a bear or tiger,' Leeuie said. 'Something a bit scary.'

'Perhaps they just chose animals they were familiar with,' Grandpa Jacob said. 'They wouldn't have had an Inter Net to research on.'

'It's internet, Mr Ortiz. One word.' Leeuie corrected. He turned back to Alex. 'So what do they know?'

Alex wasn't about to admit that she'd run away before she could question them. 'I'm not sure yet. I haven't properly had a chance to, er, chat.'

Grandpa Jacob regarded Alex with a new curiosity. 'This is certainly a turn of events, isn't it, Alice … er … Alex … ?'

'Alex,' she confirmed. She doubted he would forget her name again. In fact, she almost felt sorry for him. For all these years Grandpa Jacob had believed that he and Wilfred would be banding together to stop Kiala from wreaking havoc on the world. And in less time than it took to drive to the nearest town, he'd learned he had been wrong. His whole life. About everything.

All things considered, he actually seemed to be taking it quite well.

'Let's assume you're correct and you are the Fortieth Sun —'

'I'm pretty sure she is,' Leeuie said, wistfully. 'She can *talk* to the alpacas.'

'— what are the other skills you have? Hand-to-hand combat training? Self-defence?'

Alex shook her head slowly. 'Why would I need to know those?'

'To fight Kiala. That's what you're going to have to do.'

Alex's stomach flipped. She was expected to *fight* Kiala? Alex could barely make it through PE without bruising an elbow or stubbing a toe. How was she supposed to battle an evil spirit — and survive?

'I can teach you some moves,' Leeuie said. There was a bit too much excitement in his voice. 'I saw this show on the Discovery Channel about the history of kung-fu so I know the basics. You need to learn about balance and —'

'All in good time,' Grandpa Jacob interrupted. 'First things first. I suggest speaking to the alpacas and then heading into the forest to track down exactly where Kiala is and seeing the state of her prison.'

Alex gaped at Grandpa Jacob and any trace of pity for the old man vanished. When Leeuie had offered to go into the forest, Grandpa Jacob had made him promise not to because it was too dangerous. But he would send his only granddaughter in?

She pointed at Leeuie. 'Why can't he go and track down whatever?'

'He's not the Fortieth Sun.'

Leeuie looked as though he would've liked to be. Right this second, Alex would have happily swapped places. 'But Kiala could send a tornado or a bushfire after me,' she protested.

'She'll need some time to recharge her power after the firestorm.' Grandpa Jacob's voice was infuriatingly calm. 'So, actually, now is probably the perfect time to go.'

This did not make Alex feel any better. 'What if something else in the forest attacks me?'

'Hm.' He was thoughtful for a moment. 'I have an old rifle you could use.'

'And I've got a hunting knife,' Leeuie added, showing the knife he had used to get the splinter out of Alex's thumb. 'You can borrow it if you want.'

'This is crazy.' Alex shook her head vehemently. 'You can't make me do this!'

Grandpa Jacob frowned at her, like she had just spoken to him in another language. 'It's not your choice. It's been decided for you.' He took hold of her arm and started to lead her out of the room. 'Come on, let's go find that rifle.'

Alex looked from Grandpa Jacob to Leeuie, wide-eyed. How could they be so calm? They were sending her to her death, and they didn't even care.

'You know what?' she cried, shaking her arm free. 'Stuff your stupid prophecy!'

She elbowed her way past Leeuie, raced through the passageway and out the back door. Her mind wheeled and spun as she sprinted down the driveway and through the gate. She couldn't believe her grandfather — her own *grandfather* — cared so little about her that he would force her to go into the forest, alone. Face Kiala, alone. Die, alone. Well. She wouldn't do it. She *couldn't* do it.

If only Mum were here. She wouldn't let any of this happen.

Alex was soon out of breath, but she didn't slow or look back. She just wanted to put as much distance as she could between her and that crazy old man with his messed-up farm.

# Chapter Fourteen

When the silver car appeared around a bend in the dirt road Alex almost shouted with joy. She waved frantically. 'Mum!'

The car slowed and came to a stop. The driver's door flew open and Mum leaped out. 'What is it? What are you doing out here?'

Alex ran over and threw herself in Mum's arms. Mum hugged her tight for a second and then pulled back, cupping Alex's chin in her hand. 'Are you okay? Is Grandpa Jacob okay?'

'Grandpa Jacob's insane and I think it's dangerous for us to be here.'

Mum cocked an eyebrow. 'Dangerous?'

'I can't explain.' Alex swallowed down her frustration. 'Just please, please, please trust me. We have to leave.'

Mum held Alex at arm's length, regarding her closely. 'Yesterday you were so excited about coming, and today you can't wait to leave. I know that we got off to a rocky start, but I promise things are going to get better. Grandpa

Jacob's bark is worse than his bite.'

'Yeah?' She could feel herself getting hysterical, but didn't know how to calm down — how to convince Mum with a rational argument that they needed to get away. 'If he's so great, then how come you've never been out to visit him before? How come you never make the effort to even call him?'

'For your information,' Mum said tightly, 'he's the one who stopped talking to me. The one who stopped inviting *me*.' She took a ragged breath. 'But no matter what's happened in the past I can't just leave Grandpa Jacob here alone. Sometimes you have to put other people's needs ahead of your own.'

'What about *my* needs?' Alex shouted.

'Alex.' Mum's tone was short. 'You were given a choice for where to spend the summer and you chose to come with me. Now, if you'd like to explain what on earth you're going on about then we can work to find a solution. But otherwise …'

There was a small voice in the back of Alex's mind. *Try telling her the truth. Just try telling her the truth.*

But before Alex could even begin to form the words, the trees next to them started to sway. A gust of wind caught Alex's hair and flicked her ponytail. Her skin prickled. She looked towards the forest and, sure enough, thick clouds were starting to form above the tree line. *Oh no, no, no …*

'Mum, get in the car,' Alex said urgently. If she could

just get Mum to drive as far from the farm as possible, then maybe Kiala wouldn't be able to reach them.

Mum followed Alex's gaze, her eyes widening as she took in the sky above the forest. 'That is … what *is* that?'

Alex ran around to the passenger door and wrenched it open. The seat was piled with shopping. She shoved it aside.

Mum hadn't moved.

'Mum!' Alex shouted. 'Get in the car!'

Then, over the wind, Alex heard a noise. The blood in her veins turned to ice. The sound was low and guttural. An animalistic growl that vibrated through the ground, deep and sticky.

And whatever had made it was standing right behind her.

# CHAPTER FIFTEEN

'Did you hear that?' Mum whispered.

Hardly daring to breathe, Alex turned toward the noise. She didn't really want to see what was making it, but she had to.

It was a wild dog, and it stood only a couple of feet away. Its eyes flashed black as they locked onto Alex's. From deep in its throat, another menacing snarl gurgled.

Alex's head screamed at her to run, but she ignored it. She knew she shouldn't make any sudden movements. Nothing to make the animal think she was prey, to encourage it to attack. Not that it looked like it needed much encouragement.

The creature's short, pointed ears twitched, and brutish muscles rippled the length of its body beneath short, fox-coloured hair. Bands of darker hair wrapped over its torso and rump. Almost like tiger stripes.

The creature opened its mouth, jaw stretched wide, wide, wide. Its black gums were punctuated with sharp, triangular teeth. Black saliva, thick as molasses, leaked over its mottled lips. The animal roared. Its breath hit Alex in the face, frigid and stale.

Before Alex could stop her, Mum raced around from the other side of the car. She stopped dead in her tracks. 'Oh my … That looks like … But it can't be …'

Alex frowned. Why was Mum just standing there gaping at the dog like it was her long-lost pet? Why wasn't she trying to get away? And then, recognition sparked in Alex, too. Because this was not a wild dog.

This was a Tasmanian tiger.

But … weren't Tasmanian tigers supposed to be extinct?

'This is unbelievable.' Mum edged closer to Alex, talking in a low voice. 'No one has seen a Tasmanian tiger for, oh, seventy years. I don't understand how this is possible.'

But Alex understood. Like everything else inexplicable that had happened in the last few hours, this creature was linked to Kiala. It had to be.

The tiger's lips curled back, fur prickling in spikes on its haunches. It crouched low to the ground, eyes trained on Alex.

And then it pounced.

Everything happened in a blur. Mum hurled herself in front of the tiger. She screamed as the animal sunk its fangs into the soft flesh of her arm.

Alex grabbed the closest bag of shopping from the passenger seat and swung it as hard as she could at the tiger.

A tub of chocolate chip ice-cream caught the animal in the ribs. The tiger skidded sideways, letting go of Mum's arm.

'Get away from her!' Alex screamed. She swung the bag again and thwacked the tiger across the side of the head. She hit it again and again, until the lid flew off the ice-cream, covering the tiger in a goopy white and brown mess. The tiger mewled and cowered, pawing at its eyes before finally scampering away in the direction of the forest.

The wind dropped. The knot of steely clouds vanished. From a nearby tree, a bird cawed.

Mum was slumped on the ground. Blood pooled beneath her. Alex's chest tightened. 'Mum, wake up!' She ripped off her sweatshirt and pressed it against the gaping wound in her arm. Mum's breathing was coming in shallow bursts and her eyes were closed.

'Someone help us!' Alex screamed. But there was no one. Nothing but bushes and trees and dirt.

Alex's hands were sticky with melted ice-cream and blood. Panic clawed at her. She desperately tried to still her racing mind. She needed a plan. *What do I do … What do I do … What do I do?*

A doctor. Yes. She had to get Mum to a doctor.

She grabbed Mum's mobile and punched in the emergency number. An icon in the corner flashed 'No Service.' *No! No, no, no, no!*

A helpless sob escaped from somewhere deep inside Alex. She needed to get to the phone at Grandpa Jacob's farm.

Running here hadn't taken her long, but there was no way she was leaving Mum alone to run back. And she couldn't carry her all that way.

Alex looked at the car.

If Leeuie could drive a truck, how hard could this be?

She hooked her arms beneath Mum's and started to drag her around the vehicle. Mum was all floppy and awkward, like she was a giant doll of Mum rather than the real person. For the first time ever, Alex was grateful she had inherited Dad's lanky build, rather than Mum's diminutive one.

By the time she heaved Mum into the front passenger seat, Alex was drenched with sweat. She pulled the seatbelt tight across Mum's chest then raced around to the driver's side and buckled herself in. She gripped the steering wheel.

Alex had watched Mum drive hundreds of times before. Turn on engine, put gear stick in D, accelerate, steer, brake. She took a shaky breath. That's all there was to it, right?

The keys were still in the ignition, and the car purred to life when Alex turned them. She shoved her foot onto one of the pedals and the car shot forward, tyres churning on the dirt track. She jammed her foot on the other pedal, bringing the car to a juddering halt.

Tears streamed down Alex's face, and she angrily wiped them away. Crying wasn't going to drive the car. Crying wasn't going to get them to a phone faster.

Clutching the wheel, she inched her foot off the brake

and onto the accelerator, jerking the car along the road.

After what felt like forever, Alex finally saw Grandpa Jacob's gate. As she edged between the posts, metal scraped on metal, emitting a tinny shriek.

Alex cringed, instinctively glancing at the seat next to her, wishing Mum would wake up and tell her off. But Mum didn't open her eyes. She didn't do anything.

# CHAPTER SIXTEEN

Alex pulled up at the back of the house, behind Leeuie's truck. 'GRANDPA JACOB!'

A flock of birds in a nearby tree screeched and took to the air. Leeuie ran out of the house first, followed by Grandpa Jacob hobbling as fast as he could. They both stopped short when they saw Mum.

The colour drained from Grandpa Jacob's face.

'Kiala's controlling a tiger.' The tears were back and Alex swiped at her cheeks. 'And it tried to attack me, but Mum jumped in its way.'

Leeuie's mouth fell open. 'A tiger?'

'A Tasmanian tiger,' Alex said. She caught the look that passed between Leeuie and Grandpa Jacob.

'But they've been extinct since 1936,' Leeuie said. 'There was a show on the —'

'And I'm telling you they're not extinct,' Alex snapped, 'because one just attacked us and now Mum won't wake up!'

Between the three of them, they lifted Mum out of the

car and carried her into the house. Grandpa Jacob directed them to the darkened spare bedroom just off the hallway. Leeuie fumbled with a lamp switch and the room was flooded with warm light.

Once Mum was lying on the bed, Grandpa Jacob gingerly peeled the blood-soaked sweater away from her arm. Gaping puncture marks showed the outline of the wound, where dirt and tiny splinters of wood were stuck to the ragged edges of her skin. The bleeding had slowed, but Mum's arm was an unnatural purple colour and had swollen to almost twice its normal size.

'We need to call an ambulance,' Alex said.

'I'll do it,' said Leeuie quickly.

'No!' Grandpa Jacob put a hand on his arm to stop him. 'This isn't anything modern medicine can deal with.'

'How do you know?' Alex's voice rose hysterically. Mum needed a doctor right now! She tried to shove past Grandpa Jacob, but he held her firmly by the arm.

'Let me go!' she cried. 'I have to call an ambulance!'

He locked his eyes onto Alex's. 'Please. Trust me.'

This was the man who didn't even want Mum there in the first place. And now Mum was *dying* and he was asking Alex to trust him? She turned to Leeuie. 'Go and call one! Go!'

Leeuie fidgeted with the cuffs of his tattered shirt and looked at Grandpa Jacob, then at Mum lying in the bed. 'Um, I think we should listen to Mr Ortiz.'

'No, listen to me!' Alex was screaming now. This was like one of those bad dreams, where you're shouting for people to run and they just laugh in your face. 'Call an ambulance!'

'And what exactly are you going to say happened to her?' Grandpa Jacob's voice was low, and infuriatingly calm. 'That an extinct animal, which is somehow being kept alive by an ancient spirit, bit her and now she's in a coma?'

That pulled Alex up short. 'Of course not. But she needs help.'

'See this?' Grandpa Jacob twisted the bedside light so it was shining directly on Mum's arm. An oily black substance clung to the edges of the torn skin. It had coalesced with Mum's blood, and swirls of red and black filled each of the puncture wounds. 'This is not something you see from a normal animal bite. I suspect it's a sort of …' He searched for the right words. 'A sort of supernatural poison.'

Leeuie inhaled sharply. 'From Kiala?'

Alex recalled the viscous black saliva that had oozed from the Tasmanian tiger's mouth. She'd been too petrified at the time to think how totally nuts it was for an animal to be drooling black spit.

'Can we wash it off?' Alex asked, her voice small, but she knew the answer before Grandpa Jacob said anything.

'I'm sorry Alex,' he said gently. 'Whatever it is, it's already in her bloodstream. We're dealing with powerful ancient magic here. That's not something we can fix easily.'

Alex sagged onto the edge of the bed and didn't try to

hold back the tears that ran down her cheeks. She stared at her mum. With her eyes closed, chest rising and falling erratically and skin pale as milk, the woman in the bed barely even looked like Mum.

No one said a word until the shrill of the telephone finally pierced the silence. All three of them jumped.

'Stay here,' Grandpa Jacob said.

He hobbled out of the room and into the kitchen. 'Hello?' His voice echoed down the hall. 'Oh. Neil. Hello.'

For a second, Alex considered racing into the kitchen and snatching the phone from Grandpa Jacob's hands and demanding her uncle call an ambulance from wherever he was. But she didn't. Because a very small part of her knew that Grandpa Jacob was right, and that no doctor would be able to do anything to make Mum better.

'No, no, everything is absolutely fine here.' Grandpa Jacob's voice sounded overly cheery. 'We don't need you at all. Elina? Er, she's at the shops. Alex? Oh yes, she's having a wonderful time.'

Alex almost laughed out loud. Oh yes. Such a wonderful time …

Grandpa Jacob hung up the phone and thumped his way back down the hall. Alex could feel his eyes on her, but she didn't look up.

Grandpa Jacob cleared his throat. 'Leeuie, your parents are probably wondering where you are.'

Leeuie shrugged. 'I doubt it. I told them I'd be out for most of the day.'

'What about the rest of your deliveries?'

'You were the last,' Leeuie said, 'so I can stay and help with whatever you need.'

'That's a very nice offer,' Grandpa Jacob said firmly but kindly, 'but I think it's probably time for you to head home.'

Leeuie looked at him, pleading. 'But I've read a whole bunch of books and seen heaps of shows about —'

'None of that can help!' Alex exclaimed. She couldn't deal with his Discovery Channel philosophising right now. This was *way* bigger than anything he'd seen or read or heard. She knew it was mean, cutting him off like that, but didn't he get it? He couldn't help Mum. No one could.

'Oh. Okay.' Leeuie looked at the ground, his shoulders slumping. 'If you change your mind, just call.'

As Grandpa Jacob walked Leeuie to the back door Alex squeezed her eyes shut and willed time to rewind. Why had she tried to run away? If she had waited for just another ten minutes Mum would have got back to the farm and seen how Grandpa Jacob was trying to force Alex to go into the forest, then Mum would have taken her away from here, forever.

'This is all my fault,' she sniffed. The bed creaked under her weight as she shifted closer to her mum. 'I'm sorry.'

Mum whimpered, twisting from side to side on top of the sheets, as though she were in the middle of a bad dream.

'Mum?' Alex's breath caught. She squeezed Mum's hand.

'Are you awake?'

Mum kept fidgeting, but didn't open her eyes. Didn't respond. It took every ounce of self-control for Alex not to curl into a ball on the bed next to her and cry, and cry, and cry.

Grandpa Jacob returned and pressed a cup of tea into Alex's hands.

'Drink up. It'll make you feel better,' he said.

Alex doubted it, but she took a tentative sip anyway. The tea was sweet and milky and warmed her insides.

From his shirt pocket, Grandpa Jacob pulled a glass bottle which was filled with a purple substance. He removed the cork stopper.

Alex wrinkled her nose as a sour earthy smell, like compost and vinegar, filled the room. 'What's that?'

'In my research I've come across a lot of ancient medicine recipes,' he explained. 'Some of them better than others. This is one of the good ones.'

Alex perked up. 'You think that could fix her?'

Grandpa Jacob shook his head. 'But it should help calm her nervous system. Stop her being too agitated, in too much pain.' He hesitated, his voice catching. 'It helped your grandmother at the end far more than any of those things the doctors gave her.'

He filled a spoon, his hands shaking ever so slightly as he held it up to Mum's mouth. She twisted and fussed, unable to lie still.

'Come on,' he said in a soothing voice, the same one he'd used talking to the alpacas. 'Open up. There's a good girl.'

He managed to get the spoon between her lips and even though Mum wasn't conscious, she swallowed. Within a minute her breathing calmed and she stopped whimpering. Alex leaned closer. Mum just looked like she was peacefully asleep now. 'It's working!'

Grandpa Jacob re-corked the bottle and put it next to the bed. 'It'll buy us some time, a day or two maybe, but it can't undo what's been done to her.'

'But she looks better,' Alex said.

Grandpa Jacob shook his head sadly. 'The only antidote for magic such as this is to destroy the source it comes from.'

Then Alex understood. To fix Mum she had to reverse the effects of the poison. And that meant finding Kiala and taking the spirit's power away by putting her into a new prison.

Alex put down her mug of tea and wiped her nose on the back of her hand. 'I'll go and find out what the alpacas know.'

# CHAPTER SEVENTEEN

The sky was that specific colour of blue that you only saw in photographs. Birds and insects hummed through the air, busy and unafraid. But goosebumps pricked Alex's bare arms. She shivered. Somewhere out there was the Tasmanian tiger that had tried to kill Mum.

'You're cold,' Grandpa Jacob said. 'I'll get a coat.'

Alex rubbed at her arms even though she didn't actually feel cold. She didn't feel warm, either. Right now, she didn't feel anything.

Had it really been only yesterday that she and Mum had got on the overnight ferry in Melbourne to come to Tasmania? It felt like a million years ago. Before evil spirits, talking alpacas and extinct animals. Before an ancient poison had got into Mum's bloodstream and was killing her.

Grandpa Jacob returned a few minutes later with a jacket. It smelled of mothballs and something floral. Alex slipped it on, noticing the buttons down the front were shaped like olives. She looked over the destroyed grove. *This*

*Olive Grove Belongs to Rosa Surya Ortiz.*

'What was the deal with Grandma Rosa and olives?' Alex asked.

'Oh, she was fascinated with olives,' Grandpa Jacob said. 'With their history and how they grew. Olive trees have probably been around longer than people, you know. They are the perfect symbol of resilience, she always said. Of peace and harmony.' He sighed, lost briefly in the memory. 'She always wanted to go to Crete because there's an olive tree there that's two thousand years old. But I didn't want to leave here, even for a holiday.'

'Did you tell her about Kiala?'

'Not exactly. But she knew my tie to this land was stronger than I let on, so she never pressured me to go.' His eyes shone with tears. 'And then … it was too late.'

Grandma Rosa had died soon after Alex was born, so she had no reference for the woman who had this impact on her crotchety, stubborn old grandfather. Alex shifted uncomfortably. If he started crying again, she couldn't guarantee that she wouldn't break down and weep for weeks. 'She made olive oil?' she asked, changing the subject.

Grandpa Jacob gave a soft smile. 'Won all kinds of prizes. The cooler climate here means a longer growing period and a more robust flavour.' His smile faded as he surveyed the charred remains of the grove. 'At least she isn't here to see this now.'

Grandpa Jacob handed Alex a canvas bag full of apples. 'In case you need to grease a few palms. Or feet.'

***

The alpacas were huddled together near the barn. As Alex made her way across the paddock, she wondered what she was supposed to say to these warriors who had been transformed into animals.

She cleared her throat as she drew closer. The alpacas looked at her expectantly.

'Er, hi,' she said. 'I'm Alex.' It wasn't the greatest opening line ever, but it would have to do.

'Told you she could understand us,' the alpaca with the black coat said in a smug voice. He stepped forward, his mouth contorted into what Alex could only assume was supposed to be a welcoming smile. 'He-llo.' He spoke way too loudly, enunciating every syllable. 'My name is Ollin. O-L-L-I-N.'

'You don't need to talk to her like she's stupid,' the caramel alpaca said. She turned to Alex. 'You're not stupid, are you?'

'Um, no.' At least, she didn't think so.

'For goodness sake Lilly, I was just trying to be nice!' Ollin puckered his lips and spat a ball of saliva toward the caramel alpaca's head — which she ducked — before turning back to Alex. 'You bring apples?'

Alex nodded and showed him the bag. Ollin brayed loudly then scuffed the ground with his foot. 'Down here. Anytime you're ready.'

Alex tossed an apple on the ground. The alpaca started to savage the fruit with his teeth, spraying apple and saliva everywhere. 'Don't stop at one,' he said, between mouthfuls. 'I'm not shy.'

The chocolate-coloured alpaca sighed. 'You'll have to excuse Ollin,' she said. 'Always been ruled by his stomach. That's Lilly —'

'My name's actually Lillantha,' interjected the caramel alpaca, 'but everyone calls me Lilly.'

' — and Alvaro.'

The white alpaca with black goggles dipped his head in an odd sort of bow. 'Delighted.'

'And my name is Moraika,' the chocolate alpaca concluded.

Alex examined the alpaca curiously. Moraika. The bravest warrior there was. Her relative. The alpaca had kind brown eyes and a gentle voice. But there was also a tough no-nonsense-ness to her. She reminded Alex a bit of Mum. She'd be the first person to help you if you were in trouble, but also the first person to tell you if you were being a bit dramatic. Alex smiled, suddenly nervous. She'd never had more than a handful of relatives her entire life. And none of them were anything as cool as an ancient warrior alpaca.

Moraika smiled back. 'And you must be the person we've been waiting for all these years.'

'The Fortieth Sun. Yeah, that's me.'

'How tall are you?' Lilly asked, regarding her critically.

'Five one? Five two?'

'Um, something like that, I guess,' Alex said. Why did they need to know her height?

'Hm.' Lilly cocked her head to one side. 'I thought the Fortieth Sun would be taller.'

'Me too,' Ollin agreed around the mouthful of apple. 'And be a bit less … you know … like a kid.'

Alex flushed. 'Well I expected the Guardians would be less furry,' she shot back.

'Fair point,' Lilly conceded. 'Although technically, we're woolly not furry.'

'At any rate,' Moraika said loudly, glaring at Lilly and Ollin, 'it's wonderful to finally meet you. Although, not in the most ideal of circumstances, given that Kiala's strength is rapidly increasing. But honestly, it's a relief to finally have something useful to do. We've been waiting around a very long time!'

Alex frowned. 'About that. Grandpa Jacob said you'd only been here ten years.'

'In these bodies, yes,' Moraika explained. 'But our spirits are immortal, so when one body dies, our spirits move to another.'

'We've been all different kinds of animals,' Lilly said.

'The best was when we were snakes,' said Ollin. 'Sssssssss! No one messed with us then.' He sighed. 'But, we can't ever be the same animal twice, so here we are.'

Alex shuddered. Thank goodness they'd been through

their reptilian phase already.

'My point is,' Moraika continued, 'we're ready when you are. A thousand years is a long time to sit around waiting to do something meaningful.'

'Nine hundred and ninety years,' Lilly corrected.

'You don't know why Kiala's woken up, do you?' Alex asked. 'Grandpa Jacob said that she was meant to be asleep for another ten years.'

Moraika shook her head slowly. 'Magic isn't an exact science. But now that she's awake, we won't have long.'

'How long?' Alex asked.

Moraika looked to the others. 'Two days? Maybe three?'

'But she's getting stronger all the time,' Alvaro added. 'So the sooner we get underway the better. Is there anything other than the fire that we need to be aware of?'

Alex hastily described what had happened after the fire, leaving out the teensy detail of her freaking out about being the Fortieth Sun and running away. These warrior alpacas didn't need to know she was the reason Mum was currently lying in Grandpa Jacob's spare room, comatose. When she told them about the Tasmanian tiger, the alpacas shared the same incredulous look that Leeuie and Grandpa Jacob had.

'But haven't Tasmanian tigers been extinct since …' Moraika looked to the others for an answer.

'Nineteen thirty-six,' Lilly offered.

'Right.' Moraika frowned. 'So how is that possible?'

Alex shrugged. It didn't matter *how* it was possible. The

point was, it had happened and she needed to fix it. 'I just need to get rid of Kiala so Mum will get better.'

'Of course,' Moraika said. 'In that case, let's get started.'

Some of the weight lifted from Alex's shoulders. The alpacas knew what to do. Mum was going to be fine. *Everything* was going to be fine.

Alvaro pulled himself up to his full height. 'We're ready for your command,' he said in his booming voice.

Alex hesitated. 'What do you mean you're ready for my command?'

Moraika smiled patiently. 'You have to provide us the details of what to do.'

Alex swallowed. '*I* have to provide *you* details?'

Ollin rolled his eyes and said in a not-so-stage whisper, 'I told you. Stupid.'

Alex ignored him. When Grandpa Jacob had read out the prophecy, Alex could have sworn that the part about the Guardians referred to them as having the wisdom. They were supposed to have answers, not questions. 'Aren't you meant to tell *me* what to do?' she asked.

The alpacas looked at one another, then back at Alex.

'I'm sensing that you're a little, er, unsure about how the whole Kiala thing should play out?' Moraika said.

'I'd never even heard of Kiala before today,' Alex said. 'So, yeah, I'm a little unsure.'

An uncomfortable silence descended on the group. Eventually, Alvaro made a sound at the back of his mouth that was somewhere between a *hmmm* and an *ahhhh*.

Alex looked from one alpaca to the next. 'What? What does that mean?'

'I told you we should have written it down somewhere,' Lilly muttered. 'I told you the details would be important one day.'

# Chapter Eighteen

Alex stared at the alpacas. 'You've forgotten how to stop Kiala?'

Ollin sniffed. 'I'd like to see you try to remember something after a thousand years.'

'Nine hundred and ninety,' Lilly corrected. 'And we do remember. Sort of.'

Alvaro made the funny sound in his throat again. 'Bits and pieces at least.'

'What are the bits and pieces?' Alex said.

'You have to wake Kiala up —'

'I'm pretty sure she's already awake,' Alex interrupted.

'Well then,' Alvaro continued, 'all you have to do is extract her spirit from its current prison and bind it into a new one.'

'But you have to do it before she gets strong enough to become human again,' Ollin added. 'Because once she's human all her power will come back, and we'll be done for.'

Alex's eyebrows shot up. 'Becomes human?' Grandpa

Jacob hadn't told her that bit. 'How does she do that?'

Ollin shrugged. 'How should I know? Can I have another apple?'

Alex and the other alpacas glared at him.

'I was just asking!' he said indignantly. 'She's got a whole bag of them!'

Alex gave Ollin another apple in the slim hope it might jog his memory. 'Do you know what she's currently trapped in? Or where we find her? Or how we bind her into a new prison?'

'Whoa,' said Ollin, starting in on the new piece of fruit. 'One question at a time.'

Alex took a breath. 'What's her spirit currently trapped in?'

Ollin looked to the others, who all looked blankly back.

'It's really been a very long time since we've had to think about this,' Moraika said, sheepishly. 'And we sort of assumed you'd know everything.'

'No problem,' Alex said, trying to remain calm. Fat lot of good these supposedly wisdom-filled Guardians were. 'Where do I find the prison?'

'Oh, I know this one!' Ollin said, spraying fruit and spit everywhere. 'The forest!'

Alex grimaced and wiped damp bits of apple from her cheek. Even she knew that Kiala was in the forest. But the forest was enormous. She could spend days wandering through there and still never find the spirit. '*Where* in the forest?'

Ollin shrugged. 'Pass. Next?'

Alex exhaled a frustrated breath. 'Do you know how to bind her spirit into the new prison?'

'I know this one too!' Ollin said, excited. 'You need to use the binding incantation.'

Finally! Something specific. 'Which is?'

Ollin looked confused. 'Which is what?'

'The binding incantation,' Alex said as patiently as she could. 'What is it?'

'It's a spell,' Moraika explained. 'Each of us has been responsible for remembering one sentence of the incantation and when it's put together by you … voila!'

'Then let's do it! Now!'

'Ummm …' Moraika looked away.

Alex sighed heavily. 'You can't remember it, can you.'

She was greeted by a series of indignant snorts.

'Of course we can!'

'We'd never forget a thing like that!'

'Unbelievable! How rude!'

'Can't remember … pfffft!'

'Then what's the problem?' Alex asked, impatient.

'Well …' Lilly scuffed the ground with her foot. 'We don't know exactly which order they go in, and we *may* have forgotten the fifth line.'

'What fifth line?'

'Binding incantations always have five lines.' Lilly looked at Alex as though she really should have known this, and

Ollin mouthed 'stupid' to no one in particular.

'Why don't you just tell me the lines and we can try and work it out?'

Lilly straightened up. 'Mine is: *From the centre I arrive, striving for havoc then sleeping forever.*'

'*As black as night I ebb and flow, the currents tell me where to go,*' said Alvaro.

Moraika spoke in a clear, loud voice. '*An elixir of life that only the hero can bring forth.*'

'*As pure as light I soar and swoop,*' Ollin said dramatically. 'But, I don't know where the emphasis is, so it could be: *As* pure *as light I soar and swoop.*'

'Here we go again,' Lilly muttered under her breath.

'*As* pure *as light I soar and swoop. As pure as light I* soar *and* swoop. *As pure as light* I *soar and swoop.*'

Alex was genuinely amazed the alpacas remembered their lines at all. The sentences didn't rhyme or fit together to make a complete phrase, and there was absolutely no clue to what the elusive fifth line should be. Even after just hearing them, the words had promptly slipped straight out of Alex's mind. 'Can you say them once more. Slowly?'

'*From the centre I arrive, striving for havoc then sleeping forever.*'

'*As black as night I ebb and flow, the currents tell me where to go.*'

'*An elixir of life that only the hero can bring forth.*'

'*As pure as* light *I* soar *and* swoop.'

Alex made the alpacas say the lines over and over, until she could repeat them without mistake. The more she heard them, the more she kept thinking there was something oddly familiar about the words, but she wasn't sure if that was just because she'd now heard them about fifty times.

Alvaro clicked his tongue. 'Oh, and you can't forget about the ritual.'

'The ritual?'

He nodded. 'Yes, you must perform the ritual as you say the incantation. And to do that you need special ingredients.'

'I suppose it's too much to ask if you know what the ingredients are?' Alex said with a groan.

'The natural elements. Earth, fire, air, water.'

'But they're specific things,' Moraika cautioned, 'so you couldn't just get any old fire or water. They have to be the right ones.'

'And the right ones are …?'

The alpacas shrugged again.

Alex mulled over the patchy information. To save Mum she first had to find Kiala somewhere in the forest. Then she had to perform a binding ritual, which involved saying a spell she only partially knew and using special ingredients that could be anything related to earth, fire, wind and water. It wasn't enough to go on.

Ollin scratched his leg then yawned. 'Did we tell her about the key yet?'

'What key?' asked Alex.

'Yeah,' said Lilly, 'what key?'

'The *key* key.' Ollin sighed as they all continued to look at him with blank expressions. 'You know, the key that will unlock the mystery of the binding ritual.'

'Oh, that key,' Lilly said. 'Of course. Yes, find that and everything else will fall into place.'

'That would have been a really useful first piece of information,' Alex said impatiently. 'Where do I find the key? What does it look like?'

Lilly turned to Moraika, who looked at Alvaro, who glanced at Ollin, who grumbled, 'Why do I have to remember everything? I don't know where it is, and it just looks like the key.'

'But you must have seen it somewhere?' Alex pleaded.

Ollin furrowed his brow. 'Nothing's springing to mind.' He turned to the others. 'Do you remember seeing it recently?'

One by one, they each shook their heads.

'Not for years,' Lilly said. 'Hundreds of years maybe.'

'How am I meant to find it if I don't know what it looks like?' Alex asked.

Ollie shrugged. 'It'll have a vibe.'

'A vibe?' Alex snorted. Where did she even start looking for a key with a vibe?

A bird darted through the blue sky, chirping loudly, and a gentle breeze rippled the grass. Up at the house, the afternoon sun reflected golden and bright on the windows, making them look like mirrors.

'Have you ever been in the house?' she asked suddenly.

Ollin laughed. 'Of course not.'

'Can you imagine,' Lilly giggled, 'all of us sitting around and drinking tea.'

'Pass the milk and sugar,' Ollin said, falling about laughing. 'And let's eat some scones.'

'It's inside,' said Moraika, her eyes lighting up. 'It must be.'

That was exactly what Alex was thinking. If the alpacas hadn't seen the key outside anywhere in a really long time it had to be in the house. Alex grinned. For the first time since she had arrived at this weird place, she finally felt like something was going her way.

# CHAPTER NINETEEN

Alex found Grandpa Jacob in Mum's room. Having cleaned and bandaged Mum's arm, he had tucked a colourful quilt around her, and picked a couple of flowers from the garden, which were in a small vase on the bedside table. He appeared to have decamped half his study into the spare bedroom, too. He'd brought his desk chair in, along with most of the contents of his bookshelves, and was intently studying one of the large leather-bound books when Alex walked in.

'How did you go?' he asked, pushing his reading glasses to the top of his head. His eyes were slightly puffy and red.

'There's a binding ritual I have to do to stop Kiala.' Alex whispered, even though she was pretty sure she could have screamed at the top of her lungs and Mum wouldn't have woken up. 'But to figure out how to do it, I need the key. And I think it's in the house somewhere.' She nodded towards the books. 'What are those for?'

'Seeing if I can find anything more about this poison. No luck yet though.' He rested the open book on the bedside table, next to the flowers. 'So we're looking for a key to help you do a binding ritual?' He rubbed at his chin. 'What does this key look like?'

Alex shrugged. 'The alpacas said it has a vibe.'

Grandpa Jacob did Mum's trick of raising one eyebrow. 'A vibe?'

'That's what they said.'

Grandpa Jacob nodded once, then heaved himself out of the chair. 'Well. Okay then. I'll get the keys from the study and kitchen, and you go through the rest of the house. You can take all the keys down to the paddock and see which one has the, er, vibe.'

Before she left the room, Alex leaned down and planted a quick kiss on Mum's forehead. 'You're going to be all better soon,' Alex whispered. 'Just as soon as we find the key.'

An hour later, Alex and Grandpa Jacob had collected an impressive jumble of keys. There were keys that unlocked doors, cabinets and drawers, as well as the black stone bowl full of keys from Grandpa Jacob's desk. There were brass keys, tarnished keys, intricately patterned keys, polished keys and keys with silky tassels. Alex added car keys and Mum's house keys, which she doubted would unlock the mystical secrets of the binding ritual, but she threw them in the pile anyway.

She hurriedly dumped all the keys into the stone bowl so she could easily carry them down to the paddock.

Grandpa Jacob winced. 'Try not to break that bowl, too.

It's been in my family a very long time.'

Alex put the last of the keys in more gently. One broken family heirloom at her hands was enough for today.

***

Down at the paddock, Ollin sniffed around Alex's pockets. 'No apples?'

'I'll get some more after you tell me which key it is.'

She emptied the bowl onto the grass and, remembering Grandpa Jacob's warning, placed it to the side so the alpacas wouldn't accidentally step on it.

She held up the keys one by one. The alpacas peered at each, solemnly shaking their heads every time. Even Alex could tell some of the keys weren't right, but there were others that were big and rusty and looked as though they could definitely be the protectors of ancient secrets. But none of these even warranted a second look.

'Are you positive this isn't it?' asked Alex, holding up the one she thought was the frontrunner. This key was tarnished silver with a tassel hanging from the end and an intricate pattern on the shaft that looked like a spider's web. 'Doesn't this look even a little bit magical to you?'

'It's very pretty,' said Lilly. 'But that's not it.'

Concern flashed across Ollin's face. 'Hey, do we still get apples if none of these are right?'

Moraika and Alvaro glared at Ollin, and Lilly sent a

spitball flying at him. 'What? I was just asking.'

Disappointment gnawed at Alex. 'I must have missed some in the house.' She sighed. 'Will you look through these ones again while I check? Just in case?'

***

Grandpa Jacob thought that there might be some more keys in the back shed, so he thumped out of the bedroom and went to check. Alex perched on the edge of Mum's bed, waiting. Mum whimpered, shifting slightly in her sleep. Alex wondered if the strange medicine from Grandpa Jacob might be wearing off.

She laid her palm on her mum's forehead, which is what Mum always did when Alex was sick. Mum's skin was sticky and hot. Really hot. Too hot.

A memory from when Alex was six popped into her head. She had been lying in bed listening to Mum and Dad fight. She had decided that if they thought she was really sick, they would stop screaming at each other. She quietly went downstairs and microwaved a mug of water until it was boiling, then came back up to her room and held it against her forehead, trying to heat her skin up so she could fake a temperature. The cup was excruciatingly hot, but Alex held it there, using the pain to block out the muffled shouts coming from the other room. Eventually, when she thought her skin had heated up enough, she cried out for her parents.

When they came into her room Dad was wiping away tears, and Mum was pale and shaking. 'What's the matter, sweetheart?' Mum said, trying to sound normal.

'I don't feel well,' Alex mumbled. She wasn't lying either. Her forehead felt like it was on fire.

Dad switched on the lamp by the bed and jumped back, swearing. Alex had held the cup of boiling water on her head for so long that the skin had blistered up.

Mum and Dad had sat with her at the hospital all night, not saying a single word to each other. The burns had healed. Her parents had not.

And now Dad had a whole new family, and Alex doubted he even remembered that night, six years ago. In fact, he was probably relieved Alex had slammed the phone down on him two months back and refused to speak to him since. Less pressure for him to pretend he wanted to see her.

Tears welled again. Mum was all Alex had left. The thought of her dying was … No. Alex shook herself. That wasn't going to happen. She was going to find the key. She was going to make Mum better.

She moved to the chair vacated by Grandpa Jacob, glancing at the blue leather book he'd been reading. Like the journal that contained the prophecy, the pages were yellowed with age. Unlike the journal, which had been filled with handwritten scrawl, this was a proper printed book.

She picked it up and carefully flipped through. On the bottom of one of the pages she saw a black and white diagram of the Amarlysa, the emblem that was carved into the fence posts that Grandpa Jacob had said was the symbol of the Chodzanar tribe. A passage of text accompanied the drawing, and Alex read over it.

*The Amarlysa is considered the key to the spiritual centre of the Chodzanar people. The equal-armed cross represents the balance between destruction and regeneration, and the unbroken rings surrounding the cross and contained within it symbolise the circle of life, which the Chodzanar were chosen to protect. The four small triangles represent the natural elements: earth, fire, air, water.*

Alex read the paragraph over and over, realisation sinking in. *The key to the spiritual centre ...*

What if they were not looking for a literal key, but a symbolic key — like a picture that would help them decipher how to do the binding ritual? What if they were looking for *this* picture?

Alex gave Mum's fingers a quick squeeze and then raced out the room, the heavy book tucked under her arm. She hurtled past Grandpa Jacob, who had emerged from the back shed and was holding a handful of actual keys.

'I don't need those,' she shouted, not stopping as she ran past him toward the paddock. 'I've found the key!'

# Chapter Twenty

The alpacas scrutinised the picture of the Amarlysa closely as Alex jiggled on the spot, unable to stand still. 'Well?'

'You're definitely getting warmer,' Ollin said.

Alex stopped jiggling. 'Warmer? This isn't it?'

Ollin shook his head. 'But you're on the right track. Something else with that symbol on it is our key.' He looked to the others for confirmation, and four wooly heads bobbed in agreement.

Alex huffed out a breath. 'You could have told me I wasn't looking for an actual key.'

The black alpaca blinked. 'Sorry. Forgot.'

Alex swallowed down her frustration. Getting mad was not going to help Mum. 'Okay. So I'm looking for some other object with this symbol on it? You're positive?'

'We're mystical ancient warriors,' Ollin said. 'It's our job to be positive about these things.'

Alex barely refrained from scoffing out loud. She racked her brain, thinking about where she had seen the symbol.

'What about the fence post by the front gate? Or the one here? Could either of those be the key?'

The alpacas shook their heads.

Alex kicked at the grass, exasperated. 'I guess I'll check inside and see if I can find anything else with the Amarlysa on it.'

Moraika nodded toward the pile of scattered keys. 'Want to take those back? We don't need them anymore, and' — she held up a foot — 'we can't pick them up.'

Alex righted the stone bowl and was about to drop a handful of keys in when she stopped. She blinked. Then blinked again. Inside the bowl, at the very bottom, was a painting of the Amarlysa.

'Ha!' Ollin grinned. 'Look at that. You found it!'

Alex's heart leaped. 'This is it? You're one hundred percent sure this is the key?'

Four woolly heads leaned down and stared, then bobbed in unison. Alex felt like jumping around the paddock and shouting with happiness. They had the key! And it hadn't even been that difficult to find. Not difficult at all, really. A spark of hope flickered inside her. *Maybe stopping Kiala isn't actually going to be that hard after all.*

'What now?' she asked. 'How do we get it to work?'

Lilly shrugged and looked at Moraika, who shrugged and looked at Alvaro. He peered closer at the inside of the bowl. 'Those drawings must mean something.'

'Drawings?' Alex squinted. Sure enough, inside each of

the triangles was an intricate drawing, each about the size of Alex's thumbnail.

Alex grabbed the book and read aloud. '*The four small triangles represent the natural elements: earth, fire, wind, water.*' She looked up excitedly. 'You said the ingredients for the binding ritual are earth, air, fire and water, didn't you?'

Moraika nodded. 'Specific things, though. Not just generic earth, fire, wind, water things.'

Alex slammed the book shut, triumphantly. 'I think these pictures are going to tell us what the specific things are!'

'That's brilliant!' Moraika said. 'You're brilliant!'

The others agreed enthusiastically, and Alex flushed slightly.

'So what are they?' Ollin said impatiently.

'Well …' Alex frowned. She squinted closely at the pictures. One looked like a picture of waves with dots underneath, but if that was supposed to represent water, it wasn't clear whether it was a lake, the ocean or a river.

Another was a line drawing of a fern leaf, which could possibly represent the earth element, because ferns grew in the earth. But where was the fern plant? On the farm? In the forest? Somewhere else altogether?

The third picture looked kind of like a preschooler had been asked to draw a bow and arrow. And the last was a triangle with its pointy top missing and wavy lines filling the inside. Alex had absolutely no idea what either of those were supposed to be.

She was saved from admitting that she was still as clueless

now as she had been five minutes ago by a loud screech from above. Alex looked up to see the white eagle.

Ollin huffed, 'How would she like it if we came and stood underneath her nest and started screaming.' He stretched his neck skywards, and shouted his line from the incantation as loud as he could. '*AS PURE AS LIGHT I SOAR AND SWOOP!*'

The eagle screeched again, louder, as though this were a competition she wanted to win. Alex stopped still. She looked up. The eagle banked left, and when the sun caught its crisp, white wings, the effect was almost blinding.

'Ollin,' said Alex slowly, 'say your line again.'

'*As pure as light I soar and swoop,*' he said, dragging out each word.

Alex's mind raced. What had Leeuie said about the white eagle? That the family of them had been here forever, and their nest was hidden in the forest somewhere?

Several things fell into place. 'Each of your sentences matches one of the pictures on the bowl,' she said breathlessly. '*As pure as light I soar and swoop.*' She pointed at the image she'd thought was a fern leaf. 'This is a feather! And a feather represents wind.' She grinned at the alpacas. 'We need a feather from the white eagle for the ritual.'

Moraika whistled low. 'I think you might be onto something.'

'I'll get supplies together,' Alex said, grabbing the bowl, 'and then we can go into the forest and find the white eagle.'

'But it's getting dark already,' Ollin said.

Sure enough, the sky was a creamy golden colour, and the shadows were long on the ground. Alex had barely noticed the whole day had slipped away.

'Yeah, what about the tiger?' Lilly shivered. 'In the dark we won't be able to see if it sneaks up on us.'

'And navigation will be virtually impossible at night,' Moraika added apologetically.

Alex wanted to get underway so she could make Mum better as soon as possible. But maybe the alpacas had a point. If they got lost or attacked then she wouldn't be able to fix Mum anyway.

'Okay,' Alex said. 'First thing tomorrow we stop Kiala.'

# CHAPTER TWENTY-ONE

The last suggestions of daylight had vanished when Alex let herself quietly back into the house. Grandpa Jacob had dozed off in the chair next to Mum's bed. Dark smudges stained the skin underneath his eyes, and his brow wore a heavy crease.

Alex switched on the bedside light, and he started. 'It's so dark already.'

Alex gave him a wan smile. 'That's generally what happens when the sun goes down. How's Mum?'

'She's ...' He lifted his shoulders in a shrug. 'The same.'

In the bed, Mum shifted restlessly, moaning a little. Her breathing was still fast. Too fast.

'Should Mum have more medicine yet?' she asked.

'I don't think so,' he said. 'She should be okay for a while.'

Alex wasn't so sure. Mum seemed more restless than earlier. But she had to trust Grandpa Jacob's judgement on this one. *I'm going to the eagle first thing tomorrow,* she reminded herself. *And then I'll be able to make Mum all better.*

Grandpa Jacob rested a hand lightly on Alex's shoulder. 'Come on, I'll make us some dinner.'

The last thing Alex felt like doing was eating. What she wanted was to curl up in bed next to Mum and fall asleep for three days, then wake up and discover Kiala was nothing but an invention of her overactive imagination. But that wasn't going to happen.

In the kitchen, Grandpa Jacob sifted through the bags of groceries Mum had bought. He extracted items from one of the bags and put them on the kitchen table. A loaf of sliced white bread, a jar of Vegemite, a tub of cream cheese and a tube of honey. 'Not exactly what I'd call dinner,' he grumbled.

Alex took one look at the food and burst into tears.

Grandpa Jacob looked at her, panicked. 'What is it? What happened?'

'It's nothing,' Alex said, trying — and failing — to quell the deluge of tears. 'It's just …' She waved at the line-up on the table.

Grandpa Jacob frowned. 'You're crying about sandwich supplies?'

Alex hiccuped. 'It's the ingredients for an Alexandwich.'

'For a what?'

'An Alexandwich. A sandwich I invented.' Another hiccup interrupted her sobs. Mum barely ever let her make them at home. Not enough nutritional value, apparently. 'It's three slices of bread, the top one spread with Vegemite, the bottom with cream cheese, and then the middle spread both sides with honey.'

Grandpa Jacob wrinkled his nose. 'And you like it?'

Alex was now a bubbling mixture of snot and hiccups and spit. 'It's my favourite food in the whole world.'

Grandpa Jacob tore off a sheet of paper towel from a roll near the stove and handed it to her. He washed his hands, got a plate and a knife, and sat down next to Alex. 'Tell me how to make it.'

Talking Grandpa Jacob through how to make Alexandwiches helped calm Alex down. Afterwards, they sat at the kitchen table with the plate of sandwiches and a pot of tea. Alex took a cautious bite. Gooey honey drenched the middle slice of soft bread, clinging to the Vegemite, and squishing into the slab of cream cheese, so generous it captured a perfect impression of her teeth. Grandpa Jacob had totally nailed the triple-decker sandwich first go.

He picked up half a sandwich, nibbled at a corner and gave her a surprised smile. 'Not bad.' He took another bite, less cautious. 'So, you want to tell me what happened today? Did you find the key to unlock the secret of the binding ritual?'

Alex licked honey from her fingers and nodded to the stone bowl she had left on the table. 'It turns out that's the key.'

Grandpa Jacob's mouth fell open. 'The stone bowl from my study?'

Alex nodded and helped herself to another Alexandwich. 'See here, the Amarlysa's painted down the bottom.'

Grandpa Jacob blinked in surprise. 'I've never even seen the bowl empty before. My father always had it full of keys. So I kept it that way.'

'These other drawings show us what we need to get to perform the binding ritual.' She pointed to the picture she had originally thought was a fern leaf, but now knew was a feather. 'See this one? I need to go into the forest and get a feather from the white eagle.'

Grandpa Jacob looked at her, alarmed. 'Go into the forest?'

'First thing tomorrow morning.'

He shook his head. 'No, that's not a good idea. You shouldn't go until we know more. Until we have a plan.'

Alex didn't remind him that, only hours ago, he was ready to arm her with an old rifle and send her in there knowing even less than they did now. 'I have a plan. Get the feather from the white eagle.'

'So you know what these other drawings mean?' His brusque, overbearing tone from earlier was back. 'No? Well you need to decipher the rest of the clues. You can't just go forging into Kiala's forest. I mean, do you even know how to get to the white eagle?'

Alex didn't, but hadn't the alpacas been here for a thousand years? They had to know, surely. 'It's under control,' Alex said.

Grandpa Jacob huffed. 'I really don't think —'

But he didn't get to tell her what he thought, because from down the hall there was a sudden loud bang. They turned to each other, eyes wide, argument forgotten.

'What was that?' Alex said.

'Shhh!' Grandpa Jacob sat very still, listening. The fridge rumbled and the clock kept its steady pace.

Then, sluggish footsteps echoed down the hall. *Thump. Thump. Thump.* Grandpa Jacob stood slowly and edged around the table. He picked up the jar of Vegemite, ready to throw. The footsteps came closer until they stopped, right at the entrance to the kitchen, and a shadowy figure was silhouetted in the doorway.

# CHAPTER TWENTY-TWO

Alex raced toward the figure in the doorway. 'Mum!' She threw her arms around her and held on tight. 'Oh Mum, I'm so, so, so sorry!'

But the hug wasn't returned. Mum didn't move. Alex pulled back, puzzled. Mum just stared at a spot somewhere above Alex's head, her face expressionless, as though Alex wasn't even there.

'Mum?' Alex's voice was a whisper.

'I think she's sleepwalking,' Grandpa Jacob said in a low voice. 'Come on, Elina. Let's get you back to bed.'

Alex peered closer. Mum's eyes. They were huge pools of raven black. Unfocused. Bottomless. Exactly the same as the Tasmanian tiger.

A sob started to build deep inside Alex's chest. She grabbed Mum's hand, pleading. 'Mum. Please. You've got to wake up!'

All of a sudden, Mum jerked her hand away and hissed at Alex. 'I am awake. I am very, *very* awake.'

The voice was Mum, but not Mum. The intonation was off. And she sounded sulky. Sullen. Savage.

The sob burst out of Alex. 'It's Kiala! She's possessed Mum!'

Grandpa Jacob paled. He tried to take Mum's arm. 'Come now, Elina, you —'

Before he could finish, Mum shoved him away. She trudged towards the back door, her steps heavy and cumbersome, like she hadn't quite got the hang of this walking thing yet. Her clumsy fingers fumbled with the lock for just a second before it sprang free and the door opened. Outside, the night was endless.

Alex took hold of her arm. If she let Mum go out there — go into the forest — she would never see her again. She knew that. 'Leave my mum alone!' she shouted into the thick, unforgiving darkness.

Mum's eyes flashed. Quick as a breath, she pushed Alex, hard, slamming her against the doorframe, knocking the wind out of her. 'She's not yours anymore,' Mum snarled. 'She's mine. I own her. And it's time for her to come home.'

Alex gasped for breath. Pinpricks of light danced through her vision. Mum laughed cruelly. Hot, unwanted tears sprang to Alex's eyes. She had to remind herself that this wasn't really Mum. Mum would never behave like this. She wouldn't hurt Alex. Ever.

Mum headed down the path, away from the house.

Desperation thudded inside Alex. She had to stop Mum from going to Kiala. She needed some way of breaking the spirit's grip over her.

Then a thought struck her. The medicine!

It had calmed Mum earlier. Helped her sleep peacefully. Maybe an extra-large dose of it would be strong enough to override the grasp Kiala had over her?

Mum had already reached the back gate and was undoing the latch.

'Get the medicine!' Alex shouted at Grandpa Jacob as she took off down the path after Mum.

She launched herself onto Mum's back, wrapping her arms and legs around her mother. A roar burst from Mum's throat. She thrashed side to side with a ferocity that wasn't her own, spitting and hissing, trying to shake Alex free. Alex gripped tighter, apologising over and over again in her head. *This isn't you ... This isn't you ... This isn't you ...*

Grandpa Jacob returned and jerked the stopper out of the bottle, throwing it on the ground. 'Hold her still!'

Alex held on with all her strength as Mum twisted and fought. 'Hurry up,' Alex cried.

Grandpa Jacob thrust the neck of the bottle into Mum's mouth and tipped it upside down. He didn't release the pressure until all the medicine was gone.

Mum stopped fighting. She slithered to the ground, a dead weight. Alex fell on top of her. 'Mum? Mum!' Alex scrambled off. 'Wake up!'

Grandpa Jacob put a hand on Alex's shoulder. 'She's okay. Look.'

Mum's chest rose and fell in deep even breaths. She was asleep. Kiala was gone — for now. But the spirit's words were spinning and spinning around Alex's head. *She's not yours anymore. She's mine. I own her ... She's not yours anymore. She's mine. I own her ...*

As they carried Mum to the bedroom, Alex thought about what the alpacas had said earlier, too. They said they had to stop Kiala before she became human again. Alex had assumed that meant Kiala would just sort of ... transform. One moment she'd be a spirit, the next a person. But what if Kiala the spirit couldn't make herself human again? Her human body was gone, after all. What if she needed a new body to put her spirit into — a new 'host' — and that's why she'd infected Mum and tried to get her into the forest? The thought made Alex's stomach curdle.

She had no idea if her hunch was right, but she wasn't going to wait around to find out. She pulled the bedcovers up to Mum's chin and gave her hand a last, quick squeeze. 'I have to go now,' she said.

Grandpa Jacob frowned. 'Go where?'

'The forest,' Alex replied, her voice steady and sure. 'I'm going into the forest tonight.'

# CHAPTER TWENTY-THREE

'The forest?' Grandpa Jacob followed Alex into the kitchen. 'No. Absolutely not. Out of the question!'

Alex didn't *want* to go into the forest. But she knew she had to. 'I'll find the feather and figure out the other stuff on the way.'

'Kiala's power is too strong,' Grandpa Jacob said stubbornly. 'I won't allow it.'

'She's trying to use Mum as her human body!' Alex exclaimed. 'I have to do *something*.'

'I agree, you do have to do something.' Grandpa Jacob fixed his gaze on Alex. 'And here's what it is. You have to tell me everything you know about stopping Kiala, then you and Elina have to leave, and not come back until I have finished the job.'

Alex stared at him. Had he gone crazy? He was the one who had told her *only* the Fortieth Sun was capable of stopping the spirit. 'But I have to do the binding spell and —'

He cut her off, waving in the direction of the destroyed

grove. 'Do you honestly think you can fight something capable of that? She'll kill you!'

Alex started to protest again, but as much as she hated to admit it, Grandpa Jacob had a point. Fortieth Sun or not, Alex didn't know how on earth she was supposed to beat an ancient evil spirit who had the power to conjure storms and possess other people's bodies. Suddenly, getting as far away from Grandpa Jacob's farm as possible seemed so appealing that Alex almost agreed. But then she stopped herself.

Mum.

If they left, what would happen to her?

'We can't go,' she said. 'Not until Mum's better.'

He folded his arms across his chest. 'I'm your grandfather. This isn't a negotiation.'

'But I —'

'Alex, no.'

'But —'

'No!' He thumped the kitchen table, knocking the teapot which teetered then fell, landing straight on his fractured foot. He recoiled, whacking the cast against the chair. 'Blasted leg!' he shouted. 'Stupid, blasted, rubbishy leg!'

Alex waited for him to stop shouting and lower himself heavily onto a chair. 'You want your pills?'

He nodded, eyes squeezed shut.

She found the two identical pill bottles in the study, and selected the bottle Grandpa Jacob had used last time — the one which did not have the additional label: *Warning! May cause severe drowsiness.*

She paused.

*May cause severe drowsiness …*

She thought of the cast on his right leg. How on earth did he think he would be able to hike through the forest and battle an ancient spirit with that thing slowing him down? He couldn't. It was that simple. Her heart raced as she took the lids off both pill containers and switched the contents of the two bottles.

Back in the kitchen, she handed the bottle to him. He glanced at the label then opened the container. He shook out one pill, hesitated, then added another, swallowing the two pills quickly.

Alex's face burned. He was going to be so far beyond mad when he figured out what she'd done. But what choice did she have?

While Grandpa Jacob sat silently waiting for the pain to subside, Alex busied herself with washing the dirty teacups and plates from their makeshift dinner so she wouldn't have to make eye contact with him. Mum always said she had a terrible poker face.

After what felt like forever, he yawned widely and heaved himself up from the table. 'I'm going to get a jumper. Then I'll drive you to a motel.'

His leg thudded gingerly on the floorboards all the way to his bedroom. When he had not reappeared fifteen minutes later, Alex tiptoed down the hall and poked her head into his bedroom. He was sprawled across his bed, snoring loudly. As quietly as she could, she pulled a blanket over him and switched the light off.

Alex quickly gathered together some essentials for the trip into the forest. The stone bowl, some Alexandwiches, water and as many apples as she could carry. (She suspected midnight jaunts into scary forests would require a large number of apple bribes.) She hefted her backpack onto her shoulders. The bag weighed an absolute ton.

She stopped briefly in Mum's room, where she perched on the edge of the bed. Wisps of hair clung to Mum's damp forehead, and Alex brushed them away. She had a sudden recollection of being much younger, and of Mum stroking her hair and singing to her. Whenever Alex had been sick it was the same routine, the same soporific melody. Mum's soft singing would lull Alex into sleep and make whatever ache or pain she had melt into nothing.

Alex tried to find the shape of the music in her head. She wanted to give Mum that same sleepy, safe feeling she remembered. But she couldn't. The words, the tune … everything about the song eluded her. *Why can't I remember it? Why can't I remember the song to make Mum feel better?*

Alex sighed. Who was she kidding. A song wasn't going to fix Mum. The only thing that was going to fix Mum was stopping Kiala. And to do that, Alex needed to get to the white eagle.

# CHAPTER TWENTY-FOUR

It was after midnight by the time Alex hurried down through the paddock and knocked on the alpacas' door. Moraika nudged it open with her forehead.

'We need to go get the feather now,' Alex said, her voice low. 'Kiala possessed Mum.'

Moraika's eyes widened. She turned back inside. 'Come on,' she called. 'Up, up, up! Duty calls. No time to waste.'

'What's the quickest route to the eagle?' Alex said, once they were all gathered outside.

Ollin looked at Lilly, who turned to Alvaro, who glanced at Moraika.

'Um … that way?' Moraika bobbed her head in the general direction of the forest.

Alex groaned. 'You've been here a thousand years —'

'Nine hundred and ninety,' Lilly interjected.

'— but you don't know how to find the white eagle.'

'We've never had a need to before,' Alvaro explained.

Alex took a deep breath. Right. Time to think of a

plan B. She doubted any maps would have the nest marked on them, and she didn't want to wait until daylight in the hope the eagle would show itself so they could follow. It left her only one other option. 'Do any of you know how to get to Leeuie's farm?'

'The kid with the apples?' Ollin smacked his lips, perking up a little. 'Sure! I know a shortcut.'

Alex should have guessed the shortcut involved going directly through the apple orchards.

The Bremmer family home was a sprawling brick building, with a verandah wrapping all the way around. In the very last window, the curtains were parted and the lens of a telescope butted up against the glass pane. Alex peered inside. A small television silently played a nature documentary, the images flickering over poster-covered walls. In the single bed, a sleeping human-sized lump was wrapped in an apple-patterned quilt.

Alex tapped on the window. The shape in the bed threw off the covers and leaped up. Leeuie's hair stuck out at all angles and he blinked sleep from his eyes. Alex rapped again. Leeuie moved the telescope then pushed the window open.

In a hushed voice Alex gave him the abbreviated version of the evening's events. When she told him they needed to get to the white eagle his face split into a grin. 'Give me five minutes!' he said. 'I'll grab supplies and write a note for my parents. I'll say I'm staying at Mr Ortiz's place.'

'What if they call him?'

Leeuie shrugged. 'They won't. They trust me.'

When Leeuie climbed out of his bedroom window four minutes and forty-five seconds later, he had swapped his pyjamas for an army style jacket and trousers, and carried a backpack that was straining at the seams. His eyes sparkled with excitement as he popped his hat on his head and clipped his knife to his belt.

'Good morning!' he whispered to the alpacas, way too enthusiastically. 'It's a great day for an adventure, isn't it?' He turned to Alex. 'Hang on, do they actually know what I'm saying?'

'Uh, yeah,' Ollin said. 'We can understand everyone.' He now turned to Alex, too. 'And you can tell this boy scout to tone down the enthusiasm a bit or we're leaving him behind. It's way too early to be this chirpy.'

Alex suppressed a smile. 'Yes,' she said to Leeuie. 'They know.'

Leeuie sighed wistfully. 'I wish I could understand them. It's just all heehawing, snorting and spitting to me.'

Lilly pulled herself up to her full height. 'We do not heehaw and snort and spit!'

Ollin hocked a huge spitball over Leeuie's head, which landed on the grass with a plop.

'Okay, maybe a little bit of that last one,' Lilly said. 'But definitely not the others.'

Leeuie looked blankly at Alex. 'What'd they say?'

'Nothing,' Alex said. 'Ready?'

'Almost,' Leeuie said. He scooped up a fistful of dirt, then spat into his hand making a mucky brown paste. With two fingers, he painted stripes across his cheeks then offered the mud to Alex.

She pulled a face. 'Gross! No!'

Leeuie shrugged, unperturbed. 'The best way to stay hidden is to blend into your surroundings.' And then he started up the hill at a pace which Alex was positive she would not be able to keep up with for long.

As if reading her mind, Alvaro said, 'I can carry you on my back, if you like.'

The offer was tempting, but Alex hesitated. Alvaro was definitely tall enough to carry her and she *had* wanted to learn how to ride a horse this summer — why not an ancient warrior alpaca instead? But Alex plus her backpack was a lot of extra weight for even a warrior to carry.

'Please.' Alvaro performed his funny little bow. 'It would be my honour.'

Leeuie walked next to Lilly, casting furtive glances at the alpaca all the way up the hill. Eventually, Lilly rolled her eyes. 'Oh fine, I'll carry you.'

Leeuie looked from the alpaca to Alex. 'What'd it say?'

'She said you can get on,' Alex translated.

Leeuie scrambled onto Lilly's back, a grin on his face a mile wide. 'This is brilliant! Oooh, her wool is so soft! And her ears are so silky! And —'

'Tell him to cut that out or he's walking,' Lilly muttered.

'I'm a warrior for crying out loud, not a prize poodle.'

They walked in silence the rest of the way up the hill, until they reached the threshold of the forest. Up close, the trees looked as tall as skyscrapers, menacing and shadowy.

'Gosh, it's really quite dark in there, isn't it?' Ollin sounded nonchalant, but his tail flicked nervously from side to side.

It was. Goosebumps tingled on Alex's arms. The black and grey shapes of the forest morphed into every kind of monster Alex had ever imagined hiding under her bed. Even worse, enough time must have passed by now for Kiala to be fully recharged. The spirit would be able to attack any time she liked.

And they would never know she was coming.

# CHAPTER TWENTY–FIVE

Only slivers of moonlight managed to penetrate the canopy of foliage above. The alpacas stuck close together, walking in a tight single file behind Lilly. From his place on Lilly's back, Leeuie checked his compass every few metres, soundlessly nudging Lilly on the right course.

The near-darkness played tricks with Alex's mind. The vines crawling and twisting over each other became writhing pythons, and the pale silver eucalyptus trunks were shadowy ghost-zombies. She barely dared to breathe. Kiala could be anywhere. She could be everywhere. Each rustle of leaves sounded like a tiger attacking or the first spark of flame igniting a bushfire. *Don't think about tigers or firestorms … Don't think about tigers or firestorms … Don't think about tigers or firestorms …*

Alex tried to cram her head full of other thoughts. Like, what was going on back at the farm? Was Mum's medicine still working? Had Grandpa Jacob woken up? And just how mad was he that Alex had swapped his pills? She was relieved when watery lemon light began to seep through the canopy of trees and the monstrous shapes were revealed for what they were — ordinary branches, ferns, rocks and trunks. There was no tiger and no bushfire. In fact, the forest looked exceedingly … normal. No hint of magic or evil or myth.

Alex wasn't sure if she should be reassured or worried by this.

Suddenly, Leeuie pulled Lilly up short and jumped off her back. He crouched low and stared intently at something near the ground.

Alex's heart jolted. 'What is it?' she whispered.

'It's this plant,' Leeuie murmured, his voice urgent. 'Look at it!'

Alex peered at the shrub. It had long stalks covered with small green leaves and sprays of yellow flowers with rounded petals. It looked no different to any other shrubby-flowery-planty type thing. 'What about it?'

'I've never seen anything like it around here,' Leeuie said.

'You nearly gave me a heart attack because you don't know what some dumb plant is?' Alex hissed.

Leeuie looked hurt. 'I've memorised every native and introduced species in this area. And I'm telling you, I've never seen this before.'

Alex snorted in disbelief. 'You do not know every single plant in this forest.'

'I do so,' Leeuie said, defensively. 'What else was I meant to do last summer?'

Alex could think of a thousand things, but kept those to herself. It didn't seem smart to start insulting the only person who actually had any idea where they were supposed to be going.

Leeuie remounted Lilly, checked his compass, and led the group forward again. To prove he did indeed know every single plant in the forest, he kept up a whispered commentary on all the vegetation they passed, outlining order, family, genus and species. Alex's insistence that she *literally* did not care fell on deaf ears.

Every now and again, the yellow flowering shrub would appear on their path and it would perplex him all over again. At first, Alex felt a sense of smug delight that Leeuie was stumped by the name of this single plant, but after a while she wished he could figure it out so he would just shut up.

'Don't worry,' he said. 'When we get to the nest I can check my botany books.'

'You brought *books* with you?' Alex said incredulously.

'Just three books,' he replied, nonplussed. 'I wasn't sure if you had a plan, so I thought I should come prepared.'

Alex bristled. Of course she had a plan. Get to the white eagle. Get a feather. Behind Leeuie's back, she stuck out her tongue.

\*\*\*

They walked.

And walked.

And kept walking.

Leeuie hadn't been kidding about how far away the white eagle's nest was. Alex's bottom had gone numb from sitting on Alvaro for so long, so she slid from the alpaca's back.

Moraika quickly fell into step beside her. 'Does it strike you as odd that there haven't been any signs of Kiala yet? I'm a little worried we're walking straight into a trap.'

Alex had been thinking — or rather, trying *not* to think — the same thing. If the shoe was on the other foot, and Alex was the ancient evil spirit with serious destructive powers, she would have used her magic to wipe out the whole group hours ago.

So why hadn't Kiala done anything?

All the worst-case scenarios she'd worked so hard to damp down sprang back into her mind tenfold. It didn't help that, in this part of the forest, the overhead foliage hung low and brushed across Alex's shoulders and hair, like they were walking through spiders' webs. She was so on edge that when something nudged her backpack, she almost jumped out of her skin.

Ollin's quivering nostrils appeared over her shoulder. 'You got more apples in there?'

'You can't sneak up on people like that,' Alex hissed at him.

'And you can't expect me to go any further without

sustenance,' the alpaca shot back. 'I'm dying of starvation here.'

'We can stop when we get to the nest,' Alex said.

'When we get to the nest?' Ollin snorted. 'But I'm hungry now!'

'What's he saying?' Leeuie asked.

'He's hungry,' said Alex. 'Just for a change.'

'I'm getting a little peckish too,' Leeuie said. 'Did you bring food?'

Alex eyed Leeuie's enormous backpack. 'You brought books but you didn't bring *anything* to eat?'

Leeuie shrugged. 'No space. Besides, I thought it would give me a chance to practise all the stuff I've learned about bush tucker and living off the land.'

'Asking me for food isn't living off the land.'

He shrugged again. 'If you have some food then I won't need to live off the land. If you don't, then I will.'

They paused briefly for Alex to dole out the last of the apples and share her precious Alexandwiches with Leeuie.

Ollin swallowed his apple in three bites and was looking curiously at the Alexandwich. 'What's that?'

'A sandwich.'

'San-Dweech,' he repeated slowly. 'Is it made from apple?'

'No.'

'Can I taste it?'

'You won't like it.'

'Please,' he said. 'Pretty please?'

Alex rolled her eyes and held up a corner of the bread for him. He took a tentative nibble.

'See. Nothing like apples,' Alex said.

Ollin chewed thoughtfully. 'I think I need one more bite.'

Alex exhaled loudly then held up the sandwich again. He took a bigger mouthful, getting saliva all over the rest of the sandwich, and Alex's hand.

'Ugh, just have the whole thing.' She wiped her hand on her jeans, glowering at Ollin, but he was too busy with the 'San-Dweech' to notice.

Not for the first time today, she wondered whether coming into the forest with a half-baked plan, four alpacas and an overzealous farm boy was the worst idea she'd ever had.

And then, as if to confirm her suspicions, Leeuie called out from up ahead. 'Um, Alex? I think we're in trouble. We've reached a dead end.'

# CHAPTER TWENTY-SIX

Alex pushed her way through branches in the direction of Leeuie's voice. How could they have reached a dead end? Forests didn't have dead ends.

She found the four alpacas and Leeuie staring up at a towering wall of intertwined vegetation. A thick patch of the yellow flowering plants had grown right at the base, where they were standing. The bright, sunny colour was a cheery contrast to the sombre green of the living wall. But Alex felt anything but cheery as she looked left, then right. The wall just went on and on and on. There was no way past.

They had hit a dead end.

'We must have come the wrong way,' Alex said.

Leeuie took his hat off and scratched his head. He turned in a circle, put his hat back on, and gently tapped the compass. 'Nope, this is definitely the way to the eagle's nest.'

'Is he positive?' Moraika said doubtfully.

Leeuie frowned. 'Did she ask something?'

'She wants to know if you're positive this is the right way.'

'Absolutely.'

'One hundred percent positive?' Lilly chimed in.

'Two hundred percent positive?' Ollin added.

Leeuie looked at Alex, blankly.

'Are you *positive* positive?' Alex said.

'This is the way to get to the eagle's nest,' Leeuie said. He pointed at the centre of the green wall. 'It's just through there.'

'And how are we meant to get through there?' Alex asked, her patience wearing thin. Leeuie had promised he knew how to get to the eagle's nest. It was the reason he was here. And she didn't have time for his uncertainty. *Mum* didn't have time for it.

Leeuie unclipped his knife from his belt. 'I suppose if it's just plants we could cut our way through.' He started slicing wildly through the creepers, but the knife struck something hard. He retracted his hand quickly, shaking his wrist.

Using the blade of the knife, he pulled back the creepers to reveal solid black rock underneath. He gave Alex a weak smile. 'This knife is good, but it's not that good. Sorry.'

Alex glared. What good was sorry? Sorry was not going to stop her stomach from groaning with hunger or her shoulders from aching. Sorry was not going to get rid of Kiala. And sorry was not going to make Mum better. 'I need to find the white eagle,' she said through gritted teeth. 'I thought you said you could do that.'

'I can!' Leeuie protested. 'The nest is through there.' He

hesitated, then added in a small voice, 'Well, at least, I'm ninety-nine-point-nine percent sure it is.'

'What does that even mean?' Alex glared daggers at him. 'You told me you knew how to get to the white eagle's nest.'

'I didn't say that exactly. I told you I *thought* I knew how to get to the white eagle's nest, but I'd never actually been there.'

Alex groaned loudly. She wished the white eagle would suddenly appear and eat Leeuie for lunch so she would never have to see him again. 'So you're saying we're lost.'

'We're not lost,' Leeuie said, but he really didn't sound certain about that.

Ollin brayed loudly. 'Great! We're lost, and I'm starving!'

'Starving?' Lilly rolled her eyes. 'You just had an apple and a whole San-Dweech. That you didn't even share.'

'That was *ages* ago! I'm hungry again.'

Alvaro clicked his tongue and gave Lilly and Ollin a stern look, which they both ignored.

Alex's shoulders slumped. This was a complete disaster. Finding the white eagle was her plan — her *only* plan — for saving Mum. Find the nest and everything else would fall into place. She sank to the ground, numb. She was too tired to even cry.

Ollin collapsed dramatically next to her, legs splaying in all directions. 'If we just had something to eat it wouldn't be so dire.'

'Stop whining and have some leaves or something if

you're so hungry!' Lilly snapped.

Ollin contemplated the idea for a second, decided it was a good one, and began to nibble cautiously at one of the yellow flowering plants that were growing next to the solid rock wall.

Moraika lowered herself onto the ground next to Alex. 'We'll find another way through,' she said softly. 'It won't be a wild goose-chase.'

'It's not a wild-goose chase,' Ollin said around a mouthful of plant. 'It's a wild-eagle chase. Get it? Get it?' He laughed, spraying masticated leaves and petals all over Lilly.

'You're a *complete* idiot,' Lilly shouted, trying to shake the green and yellow specks off her coat. 'You know what? I hope those flowers are poisonous and you die a slow and painful death trapped here in the forest.'

'Poisonous?' Ollin immediately stopped chewing and turned to Alex, eyes wide. 'Quick, ask the kid if I'm going to die!'

Of course Ollin would decide to eat the only plant in the whole forest that Leeuie didn't know. Alex pointed to the flowering plant, but she couldn't bring herself to look at Leeuie. 'Does your book say if that plant's poisonous?'

'I'll check.' Leeuie unzipped his backpack. He selected a fat volume, and started flicking through, his lips forming silent words as he scanned over page after page of images and text.

Ollin stuck out his tongue, displaying half-chewed yellow

petals. 'Does my tongue look any different? Is it swelling? I feel like it's swelling.'

'Ah-ha!' Leeuie held the book up. A colour photograph of the yellow flowering bush filled half the page. '*Heimia salicifolia.*'

'Who cares what it's called,' Ollin cried. 'Ask him if I'm going to *die!*'

Alex repeated the question, with slightly less dramatic flair, and Leeuie shook his head. 'He'll be fine. It's a species of the loosestrife family with the common name of sun opener.' He slammed the book shut with a triumphant grin. 'And I was right. I've never seen it before because, according to this, it doesn't grow in Tasmania.'

It took Alex a second to process what Leeuie had just said. 'Hang on,' she said slowly, 'this plant isn't from Tasmania?'

She stared at the yellow flowering plant, running over the pieces of information in her mind. The sun opener wasn't from here. Kiala wasn't from here. What if these plants had been brought over with her? And what if they had been planted around the forest as a sort of trail — like Hansel and Gretel's breadcrumbs — leading the Fortieth Sun to … to what? She stared at the wall of foliage blocking their path, then let out a yelp.

'What?' Moraika said. 'What is it?'

'Sun opener!' Alex started to tear at the vines covering the rock wall. 'What if this isn't a dead end? What if there's some kind of secret door that the Fortieth *Sun* is supposed to find and *open*?'

The others joined in. They tore down the greenery, revealing more and more of the black rock wall.

'Hey!' Moraika ripped at a tangle of creepers with her teeth. 'Look at this!'

A thin curved line was carved into the surface of the rock. Soil was caked inside the etched surface, making it almost invisible to the naked eye. Leeuie used the sharp tip of his knife to scrape the dirt out. When he had finished they could see that the line formed a perfect circle, about the size of a small plate.

Inside the circle was the symbol of the Amarlysa.

'I guess we're in the right place,' Lilly said, 'but it doesn't look much like a door.'

'That's not a door.' Alex grinned. 'It's a lock.' She unzipped her backpack and retrieved the stone bowl. 'And I have the key!'

# Chapter Twenty-seven

Alex held her breath as she slotted the bowl into the carved line. The colour of the stone bowl matched exactly to the black rock wall. The rim of the dish slipped into place with a soft *thunk*. She stood back, waiting, every nerve and muscle tingling. For a few seconds, nothing happened. But then the ground started to rumble, a low, distant moan.

The rumbling was joined by a scraping sound as the rock in front of them began to slide sideways. Light flared from the crevice, brighter and brighter as the gap widened. Alex shielded her eyes, barely believing what was happening.

Moraika's fur bristled. 'We should be ready to run. This could be a trap.'

Alex shook her head. No, this wasn't a trap. She couldn't pinpoint exactly how she knew, but she did. It was like if someone asked her how she'd known Alexandwiches would taste so delicious. She couldn't explain it. She just knew.

Where the solid rock wall had been moments before was an arched tunnel. It looked about as long as Grandpa Jacob's hallway, but only half as wide, and just high enough to walk through without bending over.

'Can you see what's on the other side?' Alvaro asked.

Alex squinted, but the light streaming through was too much of a contrast to the gloom of the forest.

'I'll go first.' Leeuie pushed his hat firmly on his head and stepped toward the entrance. 'I'll whistle twice if it's safe to come through.'

Alex stepped in front of him, and glared. She was the Fortieth Sun. It was her mum who was sick. 'No, I'm going through first.'

She twisted the stone bowl out of its slot, clutching it tight to her chest. Then, taking a deep breath, she ducked into the tunnel.

The path was made from densely packed black soil and the curved walls and ceiling were polished rock, smooth as glass and dark as a starless night. She skimmed her fingers over the glossy surface. *I'm probably the first person to walk through here in nearly a thousand years*, she thought, awestruck.

When she emerged out the other side she straightened, blinking against the sun. Her vision took a few seconds to adjust to the light, and then her mouth fell open.

The tunnel had deposited her into a secret garden. Although, the term garden did not quite do the place justice — the circular space was easily twice as big as the sports field at Alex's school, and alive and vibrant with every colour from every paintbox she'd ever seen.

Alex inhaled deeply. The air smelled of sunshine and flowers and something just a little bit … magical.

The sun, now in the middle of the sky, bathed the garden in buttery warmth. Alex tugged her coat off as she turned in a slow circle, mouth still agape.

The colourful oasis was completely encircled by a natural stone barrier, hiding the garden from the rest of the forest. It was almost as though someone had used an ice-cream scoop to remove a huge dollop out of the centre of a gigantic mountain, and in its place, paradise had grown.

As the initial shock had worn off, she started to notice details of the space. Things that stood out. To her right was a rectangular strip of jagged black rock that ran from the ground straight up to the rim. It stood out because every other part of the rock wall was covered in lush greenery.

Off to her left, a giant eucalypt stood tall and proud, towering high above every other tree and casting crisp shadows in the midday sun.

Directly opposite the entrance tunnel, a breathtaking waterfall tumbled straight down the face of the interior wall.

And finally, a fairytale blue lake filled the middle of the garden.

Alex frowned. The longer she stared, the more she thought there was something peculiar about the space. It was too neat. Too perfect. As though it had been meticulously landscaped by a very fussy gardener, and each flower, tree, rock and plant had been put in a carefully considered location.

Very slowly, she looked down at the stone bowl in her hands, and back at the garden. Then, she gasped.

The layout of the oasis was *exactly* the same as the picture painted in the bottom of the dish. The secret garden was the Amarlysa!

'Alex?' Leeuie's voice carried through the passageway. 'You okay?'

Alex couldn't wipe the smile off her face. 'Yeah. I'm okay. Come through.'

A chorus of voices emerged from the tunnel.

'Whoa!'

'Incredible!'

'Wow!'

'You think they have food here?'

The alpacas trotted to the edge of the lake, their feet sinking into the sand as they lapped at the cool water.

'Mmmm!' Ollin gargled the liquid and spat it into the air like a fountain. 'Tastes like champagne!'

Lilly snorted. 'You don't know what champagne tastes like.'

'But I'll bet it tastes like this!'

Leeuie didn't seem capable of complete sentences. 'This is … It's just … I had no idea …'

'Oh, it gets better,' Alex said, grinning at him. She called the alpacas over, and placed the bowl on the ground. 'Check this out. The garden is a replica of the Amarlysa.'

'The garden is a replica of the Amarlysa?' Leeuie looked at the bowl, then around the garden, then at the bowl again. 'The garden *is* a replica of the Amarlysa!'

'Yup,' Alex said. 'And I think I know how to find all the elements I need for the binding ritual.'

Five voices replied at once. 'How?'

'Each line of the poem tells me *what* each element is,' Alex said. 'And then the drawings on the bowl are a sort of map. Each one tells me the place in the garden *where* each element is.'

She demonstrated by turning the bowl until the landmarks in the garden matched up with the four small diagrams on the bowl: the waterfall matched with the water; the giant tree with the feather; the jagged black rock matched with the not-quite-triangle filled with squiggly lines; and the entrance tunnel lined up with the picture of the bow and arrow.

'I'll bet you anything the eagle's nest is up the top of that tree,' Alex said, pointing to the eucalyptus. 'And we knew from Ollin's line of the poem —'

'*As pure as light I soar and swoop*,' Ollin said, just in case anyone had forgotten.

'— that we need a feather from the white eagle. The air element.'

Leeuie rifled through his bag and took out binoculars. 'You're right! I can see the eagle!'

He handed the binoculars to Alex. The giant bird was almost hidden by the dense foliage, but Alex could see it clearly through the lenses. As though it could feel Alex looking, the eagle tilted its head and stared intently at her through one eye, then it let out a piercing screech. Alex dropped the binoculars.

'We'll need to wait until she goes hunting again,' Leeuie said, retrieving the binoculars from the ground, 'and then I'll climb up and get a feather.'

'No, I'll go.' Alex glowered at him again. 'This is my job. Not yours.'

Leeuie shrugged. 'But I'll be faster. I climb trees all the time.'

'Who says I don't climb trees all the time?'

He gave Alex a sceptical once-over. 'Do you?'

Of course Alex didn't climb trees all the time! But Leeuie didn't need to know that.

'Perhaps you should go together,' Moraika said gently. 'Then if one of you gets stuck there'll be someone to help.'

Alex's face flushed. She didn't want to admit it out loud, but Moraika probably had a point. 'You can come with me,' she said to Leeuie. 'But I'm getting the feather, okay?'

'Fine,' Leeuie said, sounding slightly put out. He tapped the picture of the waves with dots underneath, and pointed across the oasis to the waterfall. 'That one must be water from the waterfall.'

'Yes,' Alex said, pulling the bowl towards her. This was

her discovery. Leeuie wasn't going to steal her thunder. 'And it matches Alvaro's part of the rhyme.'

The alpaca cleared his throat. '*As black as night I ebb and flow, the currents tell me where to go.*'

'That sounds like water to me,' Lilly said, her tail flicking excitedly. 'So those last two drawings have to point to where we find earth and fire.'

As a group, they looked from the jagged black rock to the entrance tunnel, and back again.

'But which one's which?' Lilly asked. 'Those pictures don't look anything like earth or fire to me.'

'I dunno,' Ollin said, nudging the triangular drawing with his nose. 'If you squint and turn your head like this ...' He tilted his head to the left, 'that sort of looks like a mountain with fire inside it.'

Lilly snorted. 'So, what, we have to dig a tunnel into the mountain and try not to get burned to death in the process?'

'You got any better ideas?'

'Well, yeah, I do actually ...'

Alex tuned out their bickering, staring at the pictures, willing them to reveal their secrets. She was so close — *so close!* — to finding all the elements. To making Mum better.

'What're they fighting about?' Leeuie asked, watching Lilly and Ollin snipe at each other.

'Ollin thinks the picture looks like a mountain with fire inside it,' Alex explained.

'Like a volcano?' Leeuie asked.

Alex's head flew up. 'A volcano?'

Ollin stopped mid-sentence. 'Did you just say volcano?'

Alex stared at Leeuie, the picture, then looked around the oasis. Circular in shape, surrounded by high sloping walls made from black rock, like a scoop had been taken out of the mountain …

'We're in the middle of a volcano!' Alex exclaimed.

# CHAPTER TWENTY–EIGHT

Ollin looked around nervously. 'We're in a volcano? Um, maybe we should get out of here?'

Alex shook her head. '*From the centre I arrive, striving for havoc then sleeping forever,*' she recited. 'The volcano doesn't erupt anymore.'

'Oh,' Ollin said. He hesitated. 'You sure?'

'Positive,' Alex said. 'We just need to get a bit of the volcano for the ritual.' She looked at the expanse of jagged black rock. 'A piece of that black stone, I think.'

'So,' Leeuie summarised, ticking things off on his fingers as he talked. 'A piece of black rock from the volcano is the fire element, a white feather is air, and water from the waterfall is water. Which means we should find the earth element by the entrance tunnel. What do you think it is? Dirt from the ground?'

Alex shook her head slowly. That didn't feel right. And it didn't match the picture of the bow and arrow, or the last part of the rhyme. *An elixir of life that only the hero can bring forth.* 'I'll get the other elements,' she said. 'And I'm sure I'll figure out the last one along the way.'

Leeuie jumped up. 'It'll be quicker if we divide and conquer. I can get the —'

'I said I'll get them,' Alex said, not even trying to keep the frustration out of her voice. Leeuie really needed to learn when to butt out.

'But if we —'

'No!' Alex snapped. She didn't know for sure if it mattered who actually collected the elements, but she wasn't going to chance it. What if, by letting Leeuie get even one of them, the binding incantation wouldn't work and Mum wouldn't get better? 'We can all look. But I need to be the one to choose them.'

As a group, they scoured the ground for a loose rock. They checked underneath shrubs and sifted through the loose soil, trying to find a single piece of the black volcanic stone that had come free of the wall. But there wasn't any.

Alex shaded her eyes and squinted up. The black stone wall jutted unevenly from the ground and rose at a steep angle toward the sky. Unless Leeuie had packed a jackhammer in his bag (he hadn't — Ollin had asked), the possibility of shearing a piece from the rock face seemed impossible.

'Hey Alex!' Leeuie interrupted her thoughts. 'Look at this.'

He stood right next to where the vines hung down like a

green curtain. When Alex got closer, she saw that part of the rock had been carved out.

'I think it's a sort of staircase,' Leeuie said, excited.

Alex nodded. An incredibly steep and dangerous staircase, but a staircase nevertheless. 'I guess I have to go up there,' she said, her voice wavering slightly.

Leeuie opened his mouth to say he would go, but Moraika chimed in before he could get the words out. 'I'll climb up with you, Alex.'

Alex looked sceptically from the alpaca to the stone staircase. The individual steps were narrow and smoothed with age, and looked about as alpaca-friendly as rollerskates.

'I know,' Moraika said. 'But aren't alpacas originally from the Andes? I bet climbing rocky mountains is in my DNA.'

As it turned out, Moraika did have an instinctive knack for navigating the terrain, and the alpaca bounded upwards as Alex cautiously struggled up the steps one at a time. She could barely watch as Moraika leaped from one ledge to the next. But she reminded herself that Moraika was not a regular alpaca. She was made from magic.

'Is it really true you can't die?' Alex asked.

'Not in the same ways as most creatures,' Moraika said. 'If this body gets irrevocably damaged, then my spirit will just go into another animal.' She performed an impressive leap up to the ledge above. 'The only thing that can truly kill me — kill any of us — is Kiala.'

'Well, I'm not going to let her do that,' Alex said,

determinedly hauling herself up a few more steps.

Moraika smiled. 'I know you won't. You've got warrior blood in you. I can see it.'

Alex flushed at the compliment. 'You can?'

'Absolutely,' Moraika said. She was quiet for a few moments, then asked, 'Do you have brothers or sisters? Are they like you?'

Alex hesitated for a beat too long. 'I'm an only child. Sort of.'

'Sort of?'

Alex gripped the stone step above her head. 'Well … Isaac and his girlfriend had a kid a few months ago.'

'Who's Isaac?'

'My dad.'

'Then you're a big sister? That's exciting. What's her name?'

'Luciana,' Alex muttered, trying to ignore the tightness that gripped her chest. Truth was, she *had* been excited. She had desperately wanted a brother or sister her whole life, but when Mum and Dad split up she'd given up on the idea. Then Dad told her his girlfriend was pregnant. They were having a girl. Visions filled Alex's head — teaching her new sister to ride a bike, read a book, invent her own sandwich. She immediately started saving her pocket money to buy the tiny pair of green Converse sneakers she'd seen online — the ones that matched Alex's bigger pair.

But then Dad had uninvited Alex to spend the summer

with them. He was going to be too busy looking after the new baby, he said. Now, Alex felt dumb. Stupid for thinking that Dad would still love her when he had a new daughter. One that didn't remind him of all those years of fighting and shouting. One that didn't remind him of Mum.

The tiny Converse were in the cupboard in Alex's bedroom, still in their wrapping. Alex realised she should probably throw them out when she got home.

'Yeah, well, I doubt I'll ever meet her,' she said to Moraika. 'Isaac doesn't have time for two kids.'

Moraika made a soft noise in the back of her throat that Alex took to be something like pity.

'I don't care,' Alex said quickly. 'Babies are boring. And gross.' Her face flushed again. She didn't want to talk about this anymore. 'What about you? Any brothers or sisters?'

Moraika leaped up to another rock, landing with perfect balance. She was silent for a few seconds. 'Sometimes I have these dreams. Four children, all playing together. Two boys and two girls. It feels … familiar. Like it's not really a dream, but something I used to do.' She paused. 'But I've forgotten a lot of my human memories. We all have.'

'You don't remember anything from before?' Alex asked.

'Well … snippets here and there. But not a lot.' Moraika was right near the top and waited for Alex to catch up so they could climb over the precipice together. 'I suppose it makes it easier. In a way.'

Alex took the last few steps slowly. If she could choose to forget about Dad, would she?

Right up at the peak, there was a narrow ridge that ran around the perimeter of the hidden garden. Creepers and vines had crawled up from the forest floor and tangled over themselves, camouflaging the dormant volcano from the outside world.

Alex scanned the landscape. From up here, with the trees sprawling all the way to the horizon, it seemed as though there was nothing in the world apart from this forest.

At the outer edges, the trees stood tall and straight. But closer to the centre, the foliage leaned and twisted together, a tight spiral of leaves and limbs and trunks, terrifying and impenetrable. Alex knew that's where they had to go. Because that's where Kiala was going to be.

For a few moments, as the enormity of her task washed over her, her head swam with what-ifs and doubts. But then she shook herself. She couldn't think like that. Right now, she had one job. To get a volcanic stone.

She looked down at the ledge and, sure enough, there were at least a dozen shiny rocks lined up, waiting. Alex ran her hand over each of them. The tips of her fingers fizzed and tingled ever so slightly with each stone she touched.

She eventually selected one that was a little smaller than a tennis ball because it fitted easily in her back pocket. The stone had a good weight to it. It felt solid. Right.

She smiled to herself, squared her shoulders. Her plan was going to work. She was going to stop Kiala. She was going to make Mum better. And no one else was going to get hurt.

# CHAPTER TWENTY-NINE

Almost as soon as Alex's feet hit grass, she heard Leeuie shouting. 'She's leaving! The eagle's leaving!'

Sure enough, the majestic bird had unfurled its wings and was flapping away from her nest.

'Hurry!' Leeuie called. He pulled off his boots and socks, then spat on his hands and rubbed them together, indicating for Alex to do the same. 'You'll be able to grip better.'

Alex stripped off her shoes and socks, but drew the line at spitting on herself.

The lowest hanging branch of the eucalyptus tree was just out of reach, but Leeuie jumped from the ground and managed to grip it with his arms. He swung his legs up and wrapped them around so he was hanging upside down like a sloth. Then, he twisted sideways and righted himself until he was in a sitting position, his legs hanging either side of the branch.

Alex eyed the bough above her. She was taller than Leeuie, so if he could reach it then she should be able to.

She jumped. Her fingers slipped over smooth bark before she landed on the ground again with a thud. She grimaced, then tried again, but this time her fingers just swiped at the air.

'Want me to just go up on my own?' Leeuie called down.

'No,' Alex said, glaring.

She beckoned Alvaro over. 'Can you give me a boost?'

The alpaca kneeled low to the ground and Alex clambered onto his back. She wrapped her arms around the branch, copying the movements Leeuie had made. After much huffing and puffing, she righted herself and sat facing Leeuie. 'Easy,' she said, even though it was anything but.

'One down, eleven to go,' he said. He pushed himself to standing so he was balancing on the limb, then reached up and repeated the whole manoeuvre to get to the branch above.

*Show-off.* Alex scowled, then followed.

The first few branches were not too difficult. But it wasn't long before her arms and legs were shaking, and her hands were slippery with sweat. Leeuie, on the other hand, scaled the tree with the ease of a monkey. He would pause every few branches to see if she wanted help, and even though she declined his offer each time he would wait anyway. From below, it looked as though the clusters of leaves had grown a set of legs.

Just when Alex thought she could not possibly grip another tree limb, Leeuie called from somewhere above. 'You've only got two to go. I can see the nest.'

Alex hauled herself over the last branch, grasped the one above, and dragged herself up so she was sitting directly behind Leeuie.

Up ahead, where the branch met the trunk, a tangle of reeds, twigs, sticks and pure white feathers had been engineered into a gigantic nest, so large that Alex could have easily curled up inside it to take a nap.

Alex frowned. 'What's the noise?'

Soft chirping sounds were coming from somewhere inside the nest.

Leeuie leaned forward. 'She's got chicks! One … two … five of them!' He glanced towards the sky, nervously. 'She won't like that we're so close to them.'

'Then let me get a feather so we can get out of here,' Alex said. She inched along the branch, trying to find a way to get past Leeuie and reach the crisp white feathers that were woven into the nest. 'Scoot over so I can reach.'

Leeuie was also pulling himself forward. 'It's easier if I just grab it. You think one is enough?'

'No, let me get it!'

Leeuie didn't seem to be listening because he kept moving forward.

Alex grabbed his arm, trying to stop him getting closer.

'Alex!' He wobbled precariously. 'What are you doing?'

'Don't touch them!' she said, furious. 'I told you already, it's *my* job to get the feather!' This was her mum's life he was messing with. Couldn't he see that? She leaned around him, stretching her arm, closer, closer ...

'Alex, I can't hold —' Leeuie gasped as he lurched to the right and lost his balance. He let out a panicked yelp as he slipped sideways. And then he was no longer sitting on the branch, but hanging upside down with his arms and legs wrapped around it. His hat fell from his head and disappeared somewhere below.

Alex forgot about the nest. 'Leeuie!'

'I'm slipping!' His legs skidded against the smooth bark and then he lost the grip with his feet. His lower body dropped. His arms shook as he clutched the tree branch and his legs kicked at the air below. 'I can't hold on!'

'I'm coming ... don't let go!' Alex pulled herself forward, the blood pounding in her ears drowning out the panicked cries from the alpacas below.

Gripping the branch tightly with her thighs, Alex leaned down and grabbed Leeuie's wrist, locking her fingers around his bony arm. His pulse beat out a wild rhythm against the palm of her hand. 'Kick your legs up one at time and wrap them around the branch.'

'Okay.' His voice was shaky. 'Just ... don't drop me.'

'I won't. I promise.'

He swung his left leg up. His foot swiped the air once ... twice ... three times. But on the fourth attempt his ankle hooked over the top of the branch. He grinned weakly, and Alex almost wilted with relief.

And that's when she heard it.

The screech of the white eagle.

Panic clawed at Alex. She searched the sky and saw the white speck hurtling toward them. The eagle was getting larger by the second, and the eaglets in the nest were chirping excitedly, sensing their mum was near.

'Pull me up,' Leeuie cried.

Alex clutched his wrist tighter. Her whole body was shaking from the exertion of supporting him. His skin was damp and greasy, and already slipping from her grasp. 'You're too heavy!'

Leeuie's eyes were huge and round and he was breathing way too fast. 'I'll kick my other foot up, but as soon as I do, you've got to pull me around, okay? On the count of three …'

The eagle's screech was almost deafening now it was so close.

Leeuie gulped. 'Onetwothree!'

With all his strength, he kicked his right foot up. The movement was so violent that it dislodged his left foot, and he lost the purchase he had on the branch. His body jolted. Almost in slow motion, his wrist slid through Alex's hand.

He fell.

Alex watched in silent horror as Leeuie plummeted downward. He swiped at the air, screaming as his body slammed into branches which were doing little to slow his fall.

Then a shadow fell over Alex as the sun was blocked out by a huge shape above. The eagle was right there. So close that Alex could hear the wind whistling through its feathers. A strange numbness spread through her.

*I suppose this is how it ends. We're both dead.*

And she closed her eyes, waiting to feel the sharp talons rip through her skin.

# CHAPTER THIRTY

But the eagle didn't strike.

Instead, a gust of air nearly knocked Alex sideways as the huge white bird shot past her, diving toward the ground. Alex's eyes flew open. She blinked. Had the eagle missed? Would it circle back and try again? But the bird didn't stray from its course. Then Alex realised: it was aiming for Leeuie!

The huge bird overtook him, swooping underneath just moments before he hit the earth. The alpacas ducked as the eagle pulled up sharply, missing their heads by inches, Leeuie safely on her back.

Alex let out a loud whoop, pumping her fist in the air. The eagle had saved him! She wobbled on the branch and put her hand quickly down again. She wasn't sure the eagle would be so eager to rescue two falling humans in one day.

The alpacas cheered loudly as the eagle slowed and glided low to the ground. Leeuie attempted a commando roll off her back, but ended up just tumbling onto the ground in a mess of limbs as the eagle veered up again into the sky.

He stood up, then promptly fell down again, his legs shaking too much to hold him.

As the eagle ascended back to her nest, she screeched again. The noise still jangled Alex's nerves even though she was certain the eagle wasn't there to hurt them. More than that, Alex suspected the eagle's appearances at the farm earlier were warnings. The giant bird must have known Kiala was going to attack.

The eagle flapped languidly towards the nest, landing on the branch in front of Alex. The tree juddered under its weight. Up close, the eagle was almost the same size as one of the alpacas. The eagle cocked its head and regarded Alex with a single piercing yellow eye.

'Um, thank you,' Alex said, fighting the desire to back away.

She was half-expecting the eagle to speak back — this had been the single weirdest and most terrifying twenty-four hours of Alex's life, so a talking eagle thrown into the mix wouldn't have surprised her. But the eagle didn't make a sound, and instead plucked a single feather from its back and give it to Alex. The plume was so starkly brilliant it was almost blinding in the sunlight.

'Thank you,' Alex breathed. Her fingers tingled just as they had when she found the volcanic rock.

Only then did the bird open its mouth again and let out a shriek so loud that Alex thought her eardrums might burst.

There was no mistaking the meaning: 'Now go away and leave us in peace!'

Alex did not need to be asked twice.

***

The solid ground beneath Alex's feet was the most wonderful feeling she could remember.

'Did you see that!' Alex said breathlessly. 'The eagle just came down and —'

Alvaro cleared his throat loudly. He nodded very pointedly at Leeuie, who was sitting on the ground, arms crossed, staring so intently at a patch of grass in front of him that Alex wouldn't have been totally surprised if the ground spontaneously burst into flames.

Alex frowned. 'What's the matter?'

'What's the matter?' Leeuie uncrossed his arms, then crossed them again. His freckled limbs were covered in small grazes and scratches. 'Unbelievable! You're unbelievable!'

Alex was genuinely confused. 'What?'

'I was trying to help you and you shoved me out of the tree is what!'

'I didn't shove you!' Alex exclaimed. From the look on Leeuie's face you would think she had purposefully pushed him off the branch. Which she hadn't. 'I was just trying to get the feather and you were in the way,' she said. 'But you're okay, right?'

'No thanks to you!'

'You got to fly on the white eagle.' She picked his hat up from the ground and held it out to him. 'That must have been so cool!'

'That's not the point.' He snatched the hat from her and shoved it on his head. 'The point is that you made me fall out of the tree!'

A tiny bubble of shame blossomed in Alex, but she ignored it. She had told Leeuie over and over that it was her job to get the elements. It wasn't her problem if he refused to listen. 'The prophecy says that the Fortieth Sun has to do the ritual, so *I* have to get all of the elements, or it might not work and my mum might *die*.'

'Yeah, well, you obviously don't care if the rest of us die in the process,' Leeuie shot back.

Alex sucked in a breath. Leeuie's comment stung. Of course she didn't want any of the others to get hurt. That was the last thing she wanted. How could he even think that? But didn't he understand the prophecy? Didn't he understand that this was Alex's responsibility?

She told him as much, which just made him roll his eyes.

'The prophecy only says you have the gift,' he retorted. 'That's it. End of story. Nowhere does it say that you're the only person who's allowed to touch a stupid feather.'

Moraika interrupted before Alex could snap back. 'We all want to make your mum better,' she said gently. 'But you have to let us help you.'

'So, what, now you're taking his side?' Alex immediately wished she hadn't said this out loud, because it just made Leeuie smirk triumphantly.

'I'm not taking sides,' the alpaca said calmly, 'but surely this would be easier if we all worked together? We'd have more of a chance of success, don't you think?'

Alex's face flushed crimson. She didn't know how to respond. Deep down she knew that Moraika was right. But Leeuie was so *infuriating*! It wasn't his job to find the elements. In fact, he wouldn't even be here if she hadn't invited him along.

'Just a friendly suggestion,' Lilly interjected, 'but you could try saying sorry or thank you? That often helps diffuse these sorts of situations.'

Alex ignored her. She was not going to say sorry *or* thank you to someone who was being as pig-headed as Leeuie. 'I'm going to the waterfall,' she said instead, and started to stomp off to the other side of the garden.

Alvaro cleared his throat. 'I don't think you should do that,' he said.

Alex stopped walking. 'Why not?'

'Because I don't think we've got the element correct.' Alvaro paused, thoughtful. 'I don't think it's water from the waterfall.'

'What do you mean you don't think it's water from the waterfall?' Alex repeated. 'How can it not be water?'

Alvaro cleared his throat again. 'If air is a feather and fire is volcanic rock, I doubt water is just going to be plain old water.'

'It'll be something that *represents* water,' Lilly said, catching on. 'Yeah, that makes total sense.'

'There's also the line of the binding incantation to take into account,' Alvaro continued. 'It says: *As* black *as night I ebb and flow.* And that water isn't black. It's blue.'

Alex stared at the waterfall, willing it to appear black in a certain light. But any which way she looked at it, the liquid was a similar colour to the ocean in posters advertising tropical vacations. Blue as blue as blue.

She sagged. Every single positive feeling she had from finding the rock and the feather had completely vanished, sucked away by Leeuie's anger, Moraika's gentle scolding, and now this.

'But …' Alex swallowed down a helpless groan. 'If it's not water, what else could it be?'

Alvaro hesitated, then shrugged. 'I'm sorry. I've no idea.'

# CHAPTER THIRTY-ONE

Moraika nudged Alex and gave her an encouraging smile. 'Let's take another look at the bowl. Maybe with fresh eyes we'll see something new.'

Alex had a strong sense of deja vu as they all pored over the images on the bowl once again. They said the rhymes so many times that Alex was no longer concerned with remembering the binding incantation — instead, she wondered if she would ever manage to get it out of her head.

Leeuie was still cranky and trying to pretend he wasn't the least bit interested in what they were doing, but he was the one who eventually said, 'What if you're supposed to focus on the dots underneath the waves?'

Ollin rubbed his forehead against his leg. 'He thinks there's something underneath the waterfall that we're supposed to find?'

Lilly tilted her head to the side. 'Like what?'

'Like … sand?' Moraika looked up abruptly, eyes wide. 'What if this picture *isn't* the water element at all? *As black as night I ebb and flow, the currents tell me where to go.* That could mean black sand moving with the currents.'

'And sand would make this the earth element,' Alvaro said in his deep voice.

Leeuie, who had no idea what the alpacas had just said, continued talking. 'I think you might have got them back to front and this one is the earth element, represented by sand. *As black as night* —'

Alex cut him off, still annoyed with Leeuie for a reason she couldn't quite articulate. 'Moraika already said that.'

'Fine,' Leeuie said, hurt in his voice. 'I was just trying to help.'

Alex stared at the crashing wall of water on the far side of the oasis. The liquid crested over the top of the mountain and dropped sharply down, where it fizzed and foamed into the lake below.

'Only one way to find out if we're right,' Alex said with a sigh. 'I guess I'm going swimming.'

She looked pointedly at Leeuie, almost daring him to say that he'd go instead, but he didn't. *Good*, Alex thought.

Ollin walked to the edge of the pool and stuck his head underwater. He jerked it back up immediately. 'It's freezing!' He jumped up and down on the spot, shaking his head. 'My eyeballs just froze!'

Alex started to unbutton her jeans, then hesitated. Parading around in her underwear had not been part of the job description for the Fortieth Sun.

'What are you waiting for?' Ollin said, still shaking his head. 'It's not getting any warmer.'

Alex flushed. 'I can't exactly go swimming in my clothes, so …'

'Like we care,' Ollin snorted. 'We've been running around naked for a thousand years.'

'Nine hundred and ninety,' Lilly corrected.

'Yeah, but ,..' Alex glanced at Leeuie.

'Oh please.' Leeuie gave her a scornful look. 'Like I care about seeing your undies!'

This made Alex feel stupid as well as embarrassed. She quickly shimmied out of her jeans, then jogged to the edge of the lake. A shallow ledge, about knee deep, lined the inside lip before the bank dropped away sharply. Alex stepped into the water and winced. Ollin was right. Her legs had already started going numb.

'Oh, hang on,' she said, her teeth starting to chatter. 'If there's sand there, I need something to put it in. Can one of you grab a ziplock bag from my backpack?'

The alpacas looked at Alex's backpack, then at each other, then at Leeuie. 'We're not so good with zippers,' Moraika said, holding up a foot so Leeuie would understand.

Leeuie handed Alex the small plastic bag without making eye contact. Lilly mouthed 'Thank you, Leeuie' to Alex.

Alex glowered at the alpaca and snatched the bag. 'Thanks,' she said, her voice deadpan.

The bag had contained her Alexandwiches, so she

shook out the crumbs and tucked it tightly into the elastic waistband of her knickers before taking a few quick breaths and diving under the surface. The freezing water pressed at her skull so tightly she thought her head might explode. She popped back up and gasped, clutching at her temples. Worst brain freeze ever!

She swam across the lake in short, sharp strokes. It was about as big as the pool she had done swimming lessons in every summer until she was eight, but the fact she couldn't see the bottom, and didn't know if anything lived down there, made it feel ten times bigger. Every shadow or movement of the water sent her pulse racing a little bit faster, and she pushed away the thought that it might be less scary if someone had come in with her.

*Don't think about tigers or firestorms ... Don't think about tigers or firestorms ... Don't think about tigers or firestorms ... Or octopuses! Or piranhas!*

She picked up the pace. Did Tasmania have piranhas? Alex certainly didn't want to find out.

She glanced back and saw the others standing on the edge of the lake watching her intently. There was a part of her that felt a lot safer knowing that five sets of eyes were scrutinising her every move, and if anything happened they would help. Although ... Alex frowned. Could alpacas even swim?

She kept going until she was right at the bottom of the waterfall. Up close, the noise was deafening. A thunderous rush of liquid tumbling over rocks and smashing into the lake. Alex peered down, trying to see if there was black sand beneath her, but she couldn't make out the bottom.

She took a couple of deep breaths and dived, kicking downwards. When her lungs started to scream she burst back up, batting the surface and gulping huge mouthfuls of air. She hadn't even seen the bottom, let alone touched it.

She swam erratically in circles, trying to stay warm. If Moraika was right and sand underneath the waterfall was the earth element — and Alex *really* hoped she was — then there had to be a way to get to it.

And if she could not swim to the bottom of the lake, then there must be another way. 'But what is it?' she muttered, staring at the waterfall.

This close, the curtain of water looked gauzy. So thin it was almost translucent.

She blinked. Swiped water from her face. Were her eyes playing tricks on her? She swam closer, squinting against the spray. No, she was right. The water tumbling from the rocks above was nothing more than a sheer sheet of liquid, no thicker than a book.

And hidden behind it was a cave.

# Chapter Thirty-two

Alex's head buzzed from the discovery. Where better to hide one of the binding ritual elements than in a secret cave?

Without a second thought, she ducked under the surface, propelling herself forward and beneath the waterfall.

When she popped back up again, she was inside the cave.

Only a small amount of light filtered through from outside, and Alex had to wait for a few moments as her eyes adjusted. In here, the sound of rushing water was muted and a dank, musty odour hung in the air.

When she could see properly, she discovered the cave walls were no further apart than her bedroom back home. But unlike her bedroom at home, the walls here curved in, and the ceiling funnelled upwards, getting narrower and narrower, until it disappeared into blackness.

Alex's fingers were almost numb from the cold as she swam around the perimeter, running her hand along the smooth rock walls, willing the secret space to reveal whatever it was hiding. Then, right at the back of the cave, she felt a crevice cut into the rock. The hole was rectangular and big enough to slide her hand almost all the way in before her fingers hit rock again.

Glancing up, she could make out several more holes, one on top of the other, before it became pitch black and she couldn't see any further. Underwater, she pushed her feet against the wall and felt around with her toes. Yep. More holes, just in the right places for her feet. That meant more climbing.

Alex groaned out loud. The noise bounced off the walls and echoed spookily back at her, over and over.

Then, there was a loud splash, and a head burst from the water.

Alex screamed. 'Leeuie! You nearly gave me a heart attack!'

'You just disappeared under the water and when you didn't come up again we thought ...' Leeuie took a shaky breath. 'But you're okay. That's good.' He took a few moments to catch his breath, and then said, 'I'll just wave at the others to let them know we're okay.'

He ducked under the waterfall again. Alex felt extremely guilty for not even considering what the others might have been thinking when she had vanished underwater.

When Leeuie was back a few moments later, Alex told him about the ladder carved into the wall and her suspicion about yet more climbing. As she talked, she realised she was grateful for his company. Doing all of this alone was hard.

And it wasn't that having Leeuie there made it easier, exactly, but it did make it less … lonely. And frightening.

'Hey Leeuie,' Alex asked, keeping her voice light. 'Don't suppose you want to come up there with me?'

'Only if you want the help,' Leeuie said, his voice equally casual.

'Yeah,' Alex said, swimming towards the ladder. 'The help would be good. Really, *really* good.'

She could practically feel the grin that Leeuie was trying to suppress. 'Cool. No problem.'

Alex peered uncertainly into the gloom above. 'So, ah, do you want to go first?'

Leeuie snorted. 'I don't think so! You're the Fortieth Sun. This is your job, remember?'

\*\*\*

The rock holes were rough and serrated, slicing into her freezing hands and feet as though Alex was clutching at cheese graters. As she got higher, the space grew smaller, until she felt like she was inching her way through a wormhole in the rock. The passage became suffocatingly narrow and Alex's breathing came out ragged and fast. How much further could she go without getting stuck?

'Are you near the top?' Leeuie called. He didn't sound like he was enjoying this much, either.

'I don't know, I can't see —' Her head thumped against

solid rock. Blinding pain gripped her skull. She swallowed down a surge of irrational anger toward the ceiling. 'Yeah, I'm here.'

She fumbled around above her and, just to her left, found a bigger hole. Careful not to hit her head again, she lifted herself up a fraction and peered through the gap. This crevice was much bigger than the hand and footholds, and she could see a tiny slice of light peeping through the other end.

She wriggled her head and shoulders through the gap in the rock and was stuck for one terrifying second before she pushed face-first through a veil of damp foliage hanging across the hole. She inched her way out and stood up. She stretched her arms and legs, then jogged on the spot, trying to work feeling back into her freezing limbs. If she'd thought being in the water was cold, being out of it was even worse. Moments later, Leeuie emerged behind her, blue-tinged and shivering.

They were in another stone cavern, but this one was right at the top of the waterfall. The liquid tumbling over the mouth of the cave was a constant rumble, hiding the entrance from the outside world.

Next to the sheet of falling water was a narrow ledge, leading out of the cave. Alex and Leeuie pressed their backs against the wall and edged along, past the tumbling water and out into the sunshine.

They blinked against the glare, getting their bearings.

The rock shelf was wide enough for them to stand side by side, but only a few inches longer than their feet. Alex kept one hand firmly planted on the wall behind her as she peered gingerly over the edge. The lake below seemed absolutely miles away and, huddled together near the bank, the alpacas looked very, very small.

'I think we've gotta jump,' Leeuie said, shouting above the noise of the waterfall.

Alex nodded glumly. That was exactly what she thought, too. Jumping from this height would propel them to the bottom of the lake and they would be able to find the dots beneath the waves.

But what was it people said about jumping into water from ridiculous heights? Oh yeah. If you landed the wrong way, it was like smashing into a concrete floor.

'Do we go together?' Even Leeuie sounded a bit shaky. 'Or one at a time?'

'One at a time.' Alex did not fancy accidentally bumping heads in midair and then tumbling unconscious to the bottom of the lake.

Leeuie glanced at Alex. 'I'll go first?'

Alex hesitated. It should probably be her but she couldn't quite bring herself to say so. Leeuie took her silence to be a yes. He edged forward. 'Okay.'

'Leeuie!' Alex blurted out. 'I'm sorry about before. I promise I didn't mean to push you out of the tree.'

'I know,' Leeuie said, glancing over his shoulder and

giving her a small smile. 'And I'm sorry I got mad and said you did.' He moved his toes right to the edge. 'One, two …' His hands were balled into tight fists, knuckles strained white. 'Three!'

He leaped from the ledge, limbs flailing as he hurtled toward the water. 'AHHHHHHH!'

Alex forced herself to keep her eyes open and watch him all the way down. White foam erupted where he hit the lake. And then he was gone.

Alex waited. She hadn't intended to count the seconds that he stayed under, but when she reached sixty, she started to panic.

She was about to jump herself when he finally burst through the surface, gulping and gasping, arms thrashing at the water. The breath Alex had been holding came out as a joyful gasp. He looked up. Even from this height, Alex could see him shaking his head.

He hadn't managed to reach the bottom.

Alex edged toward the lip of the platform. Her legs shook, and she was finding it difficult to breathe. Leeuie had been under for a full minute and hadn't reached the bottom. Alex didn't even think she could hold her breath for forty-five seconds, let alone a full minute. She would have to get deeper into the lake, faster. And that meant …

She was going to have to dive.

Last summer, as a dare, Alex had dived from the high board at the local pool. Afterwards, she had pretended it was no big deal, but it had been so terrifying that she had gone straight into the bathrooms and thrown up. Twice.

'Okay,' she muttered. 'No problem. Piece of cake. Easy-peasy.' She focused on a trajectory away from the waterfall and, with the plastic sandwich bag clasped tightly between her hands, held her arms straight above her head so they — and not her skull — would break the water first. 'On the count of three …' she muttered. 'One … two … three …'

She counted to six.

Then fifteen.

Then twenty-two.

'Ugh!' she scowled, frustrated. 'Just go already!'

But her body wouldn't cooperate. The part of her brain that controlled *not* doing stupid things was unwilling to let her dive from a ridiculously high rock platform next to a pounding wall of water.

Alex closed her eyes and concentrated. An image of Mum's face filled her mind. Alex took a long, slow breath, holding tight to the picture of Mum in her head. *You have to do this*, Alex told herself. *You have to do this for Mum.*

So she did.

# CHAPTER THIRTY-THREE

Alex felt like she was travelling through the air in slow motion, arms held straight above her head, legs taut. Her stomach had been left somewhere near the top of the waterfall, and she forgot for a second what she was doing or where she was going, feeling the wind rushing around her until … SPLASH!

Her limbs sprang into action. She kicked down and down, deeper into the belly of the lake. The water around her went from blue to grey to the colour of Grandpa Jacob's strong pots of tea. She stroked down, unable to see more than a foot in front of her, and just when she wondered if this lake even had a bottom, her fingers sank into something grainy and soft.

Sand!

She grabbed a fistful. Her hand tingled as the grains sifted through her fingers, floating weightlessly in the water. She wrestled to open the plastic bag, then kicked down once more, dragging the opening across the bottom of the lake and filling it with sand. Her lungs screamed and her chest felt like it was being squeezed from every angle.

*I need air. Now.*

She flipped around, shoving her feet hard against the sand and rocketing towards the surface. She clutched the bag tightly in one hand, frog-kicking ferociously. It seemed like the water was getting lighter, but she couldn't tell if it was because she was close to the surface or because the pinpricks of light in the corners of her eyes were clouding her vision. Hysteria swelled in her chest. Air bubbled out of her nose. Time slowed down. For one glorious second, the lake was filled with a thousand twinkling stars. Then everything went dark.

\*\*\*

Music.

Someone was singing.

The song teased the edge of Alex's consciousness. *What is that?* A song Alex knew ... a song she had not heard since ... since when?

Then Mum was there, her image glimmering, her voice soothing and calm as the familiar melody streamed from her.

*As pure as light, I soar and swoop.*

*From the centre I arrive, striving for havoc then sleeping forever.*

*As black as night I ebb and flow, the currents tell me where to go.*

*An elixir of life that only the hero can bring forth.*
*With love I release you from your destiny.*

Alex remembered. That was the song Mum used to sing to her when she was sick, the song that always made her feel better. Alex frowned. But … she wasn't sick now, was she? So why was Mum singing it?

Alex racked her brain. The answer was *right* there. She should know this. Because … because … something important … something she needed to remember …

And then, suddenly, Mum was ripped away, replaced by a blazing white light which came at Alex from all directions. *No!* Alex wanted to cry out. *Come back!*

But instead of words, water spewed from her mouth. She heaved, again and again, coughing and retching. Her nose and throat burned, scorched and raw.

Other sensations returned. The grass beneath her back, springy and a little bit prickly. The sun, deliciously warm. And the air! The amazing, incredible air! Alex filled her lungs, again and again, as though she'd never be able to get enough.

Then she heard a voice. 'Oh, thank goodness.'

Groggy, Alex opened her eyes. The blinding white light transformed into four woolly heads, all different colours, and one mop of dripping sandy brown hair, all staring down at her. Their names manifested somewhere in the far reaches of her brain. *Alvaro … Ollin … Lilly … Moraika … Leeuie.* She tried to talk, ask where she was and why they were all staring at her, but she just started coughing again.

'That was epic!' Ollin exclaimed, flopping dramatically onto the grass. 'When you didn't come up we all thought you were a goner for sure!'

'But then Leeuie jumped in the water!' Lilly exclaimed. 'And he dragged you out!'

Ollin let out a low whistle. 'Just in time, too.'

And then Alex remembered. She had dived from the top of the waterfall. She had been *drowning*! And Leeuie had jumped into the lake and saved her. The rush of realisation startled her. If Leeuie hadn't been here, she would be dead. Then no one would be able to save Mum. Kiala would become human once more. And who knew what she would do to Grandpa Jacob, to the alpacas, to Leeuie ... to the world!

Alex clutched Leeuie's hand. 'Thank you, thank you, thank you,' she croaked, before hacking coughs overtook her body again.

Leeuie flushed and shrugged his shoulders. 'No biggie.'

Lilly's voice interrupted her thoughts. 'Was there anything down the bottom?'

The sand! Even without looking, Alex could feel she was no longer holding the plastic bag she'd filled. Her stomach plummeted.

But Leeuie held up the plastic ziplock bag half-filled with wet, midnight-black sand. 'It was floating in the water next to you.'

Alvaro smiled. '*As black as night I ebb and flow, the currents tell me where to go.*'

'Alex, you did it,' Moraika said proudly.

The vision of Mum from the bottom of the lake came back to Alex then. Mum singing. 'And I know what the last line of the binding incantation is, too,' she croaked, managing not to cough this time.

Lilly and Ollin spoke at once.

'How?'

'What is it?'

'Let the girl catch her breath for a minute!' Moraika chastised.

Alvaro cleared his throat. His wide-eyed gaze was fixated on something in the distance. 'I don't know if we have that long …'

At the top of the black volcanic mountain, at the very place Alex and Moraika had found the rock, was a pack of Tasmanian tigers, terrifying silhouettes against the fading sky.

'There's more than one of them?' Lilly exclaimed. 'I thought you said there was only one!'

'I thought there was,' Alex said.

Leeuie gulped. 'You know, Tasmanian tigers aren't actually supposed to be vicious. They're meant to be shy. Scared of humans.'

'Not these ones,' Alex said. 'They're totally under Kiala's control. They want to destroy us.' Somehow, she managed to find the energy to scramble up and pull on her clothes.

'We need to get out of here. Now!'

The tigers started to move. They advanced as an army would, together and with intimidating precision. They were slow at first, but gained speed as they got lower to the ground.

'We need to get to the tunnel,' Moraika said. 'Then we can lose them in the forest.'

Leeuie helped Alex clamber onto Alvaro's back, and he jumped onto Lilly's. The group thundered towards the entrance tunnel at the same time as the tigers reached the ground of the secret garden.

'We'll never be able to outrun them!' Ollin called.

Moraika slowed and peeled away from the group. 'You go! I'll distract them.'

'Are you crazy?' Alex cried.

Moraika shook her head. 'Ollin's right. They're too fast.'

'I'm never right,' Ollin said, looking back in horror as Moraika ran the wrong way, towards the tigers. 'Moraika! I'm never right!'

'Yeah, he's never right!' Lilly cried, not breaking stride. 'Come with us! We'll be fine!'

But Moraika had stopped running altogether. 'I'll catch up with you.' She caught Alvaro's gaze. 'Keep her safe.'

Alvaro hesitated for only a second, and then with one last look at Moraika, he raced away.

Alex turned, watching the tigers encircle Moraika. The lone alpaca raised up on her hind legs, and as the last rays of the afternoon sun glistened off her chocolate coat, she almost looked like she was made of solid gold.

'We can't leave her!' Alex shouted. The tigers had Kiala's poison flowing through them. They were made from Kiala. So unlike a normal animal, they could actually kill Moraika — destroy her spirit. 'She'll die!'

But then Alvaro was at the tunnel and Alex had to flatten herself against him, and she could see no more. She clung tightly to his neck, squeezing her eyes shut to stop the tears.

The alpacas ran and ran until finally Alvaro slowed to a brisk walk. 'I think we've lost them,' he wheezed. 'You can loosen your grip.'

Alex tumbled off the alpaca's back and began marching back in the direction they had just come. 'I can't believe you just left her!' Alex called over her shoulder. 'Those things'll kill her! Don't you even care!'

Alvaro trotted in front of her, blocking her path. 'Of course I care!' His voice had a hardness to it Alex hadn't heard before. 'But she is a warrior. She made a difficult decision in order to protect what matters — you.'

'I don't want anyone to die because of me!' Alex cried.

Alvaro's voice softened. 'Of course you don't. And I don't think anyone will.' He nudged Alex's shoulder gently. 'I may not remember much from our past lives, but I do remember one thing. Moraika was the bravest warrior that ever lived. If anyone can best those tigers, it's her. And *when* she makes it past them all, she'll find us again. You'll see.'

'Really?' Alex sniffed.

Alvaro nodded. 'She's a true hero.' He gave Alex a lopsided smile. 'I think they even invented the word hero just for her.'

'What?' Alex stopped walking again.

Alvaro flicked his tail. 'Alex, we really must keep moving.'

Alex's mind whirled and popped as all the pieces of the binding ritual suddenly fell into place. 'I know what the last element is,' she said. 'We need to find Moraika and then I can perform the ritual!'

# CHAPTER THIRTY–FOUR

Alvaro whistled low to get Ollin and Lilly's attention. Ollin stopped walking so abruptly that Lilly ran into the back of him, and Leeuie almost fell off her.

'What's going on?' Leeuie said, eyes darting about, hand on the hilt of his knife.

'I figured out what the missing element is,' said Alex.

'You did?' said Leeuie.

'Well …?' Ollin tapped his foot impatiently. 'What is it?'

'Moraika's blood,' Alex said.

They all gaped at her.

'You're going to kill Moraika?' Ollin exclaimed.

'No!' Alex cried. 'Of course not.'

'Oh.' He looked relieved. 'How do you figure it's her blood?'

'It was the location of the last element that was really confusing us,' said Alex. 'The bowl pointed to the entry path but there was nothing there. Nothing except us, going in and out.'

'It's telling us to look at ourselves?' Ollin scratched his leg against a tree. 'I don't get it.'

'Moraika's part of the rhyme is: *An elixir of life that only the hero can bring forth.*'

'Yes!' Leeuie's eyes lit up. 'Blood's made from plasma and cells, but also contains other things, like clotting agents and hormones and …'

Alex cleared her throat.

'Right. Sorry. I saw something on the Discovery Channel. But you're right! Blood is a mixture of things. An elixir! And it's *the* elixir of life because without it, well, we'd be dead.'

Alex nodded. 'But it can't just be the blood of anyone. It's the blood of the hero.' She turned to Alvaro. 'And you just said that Moraika was a hero.'

'She is!' Leeuie agreed, excitedly. 'Mr Ortiz said it too, remember? That his ancestor, Moraika, was the bravest and most heroic warrior of the Chodzanar tribe.'

'Hero is such a subjective measure,' Ollin said. 'I mean, one person's heroics are another person's —' A sideways kick from Lilly shut him up.

Alex grinned. '*An elixir of life that only the hero can bring forth.* It's Moraika's blood. It has to be.'

Lilly nodded her head slowly. 'You know, that actually makes sense.'

'Indeed it does,' Alvaro agreed.

'And back by the lake you said you knew the final line of

the binding incantation, too?' Leeuie pressed.

Alex explained the vision she had at the bottom of the lake, where Mum was singing the familiar song. 'When you first said the lines of the binding incantation to me, I thought they sounded familiar,' she explained, 'but I wasn't sure. But they're the lines of a song that Mum used to sing me when I was a little kid.'

Lilly's woolly brow crinkled. 'Your mum used to sing you a song about an ancient spirit who liked killing people?'

'I don't think she knew that's what it was about,' Alex said. 'She probably heard it from her dad. Or her grandfather. It would have been one of those things that gets passed down through the family and no one knows why.'

Leeuie's face was alight with nervous excitement. 'So … we just need to find Moraika, then get to Kiala, and you'll be able to do the binding ritual?'

Alex hesitated. Theoretically, Leeuie was right. They as good as had all four elements — the volcanic rock, the white feather, the black sand and Moraika's blood — and she knew the fifth line of the binding incantation. How Alex was supposed to actually *do* the ritual, she had no idea. But, everything else had come to her, so she just had to believe that this would too. 'Yes,' she said, squaring her shoulders. 'I can do the ritual.'

'If you're sure,' Alvaro said, 'that's enough for me.'

A branch rustled. They all froze. Leeuie put a finger to

his lips. 'Don't make a sound,' he whispered, his voice barely audible.

A second later, Moraika crashed through the foliage, her coat wet with sweat. She had a streak of blood across one thigh.

Alex threw her arms around the alpaca. 'You're okay!'

'I told you she would be,' Alvaro said, but the relief on his face was obvious.

'How did you get away?' Alex asked, eyeing the injuries, which she was relieved to see were mostly surface wounds.

'Their bark was a lot worse than their bite,' Moraika panted. 'Once I'd kicked a few of them away, the others ran off. But that doesn't mean we should be standing around here waiting for them to come back with reinforcements. Why aren't you heading back to the farm?'

\*\*\*

Using his compass as a guide, Leeuie led the group deeper into the centre of the forest. As they walked, Moraika listened with increasing surprise as Alex told her that her blood was a key part of the binding spell. 'Guess it's lucky I've got some handy,' she said.

Alex eyed the slash on the alpaca's leg. 'Does it hurt?'

'Not even a little,' Moraika said, but she was limping ever so slightly as they walked.

Despite Moraika's insistence that the tigers looked more

dangerous than they were, it didn't sound like the beasts had given up trying to find the group. Scowls and roars and scuffles travelled through the forest, coming from one direction, then another. Each time, Leeuie shifted course, so they were always heading away from the noises.

Alex's pulse increased steadily with every step she took. As they got closer to the middle of the forest, trees and shrubs became hideous entanglements of bark and leaves and branches. She had little concept of how long they'd been walking when Leeuie leaned over and whispered, 'We're pretty much in the centre. How will we recognise Kiala's prison?'

'We just will,' Alex said. Evil like that left a scar. All they had to do was find it.

And then, the dense wilderness fell away, and they were on the edge of a large clearing, in the middle of which a huge sprawling tree twisted up from the ground.

The tree's roots spread in all directions, poking through the earth in undulating wooden waves. The trunk was gnarled and ragged, and knotted branches stretched to the sky.

This was it. This tree was Kiala's prison.

Alex stepped into the clearing. She expected the ground to collapse beneath her, or lightning to rain down. But it didn't. Nothing happened.

She slowly picked her way over the exposed roots and freshly fallen leaves that littered the ground.

Up close, she could see the trunk of the tree was smooth

and grey, the leaves muted green. So familiar. So much like ...

'It's an olive tree,' Alex said in a low voice. It was the biggest, ugliest one she had ever seen but, without a doubt, an olive tree.

Alex recalled what Grandpa Jacob had said about the olives. That they could live for thousands of years. That they represented resilience, peace and harmony.

When you put it like that, they were the perfect prison for a spirit of destruction. And Kiala knew it. That's why she destroyed the olive grove. She was trying to get rid of them all.

'Look at this.' Leeuie pointed to the bottom of the trunk, which had been clawed and scratched and bitten so it was a mess of lacerated, splintered wood. A black, viscous substance oozed out, bubbling to the surface like beads of oily sweat.

Leeuie reached out to touch it.

'Don't!' Alex hit his hand away. That was the same substance that had been dripping from the jaws of the tiger that had bitten Mum. 'That's how she controls the Tasmanian tigers. They get that in their system and they do whatever she wants.'

'That's how she's been keeping them alive this whole time?' Leeuie asked.

'I don't think she's exactly keeping them alive,' Alex said, slowly. Kiala was the spirit of *destruction*, after all. 'I think they're probably in some kind of ... in-between state. Not alive, not dead. And she controls if they deteriorate or not.'

'But that means she's kept them hidden for over eighty years,' Leeuie said. 'What's she been waiting for?'

With a shake of her head, Alex dismissed the question. That didn't matter. In a few minutes, after she had performed the binding ritual, Mum would get better and life would go back to the way it was. Kiala would once again be rendered powerless.

A deep growl from the forest made Alex whip around. Scores of glowing eyes shone through the darkness as the Tasmanian tigers surrounded the clearing. Every single hair on Alex's body sprung to attention, and she leaped from the ground, grabbing her backpack close.

'I thought we'd lost them,' Ollin said. He backed slowly away. 'I thought we'd managed to get away.'

The tigers stalked forward, slow and purposeful, shepherding the group closer together. Closer to the tree. The alpacas huddled around Alex and Leeuie, tails flicking, eyes darting from one tiger to the next.

Leeuie blanched. 'I don't think we were ever running away from them,' he said in a hoarse voice. 'I think they were herding us.'

# CHAPTER THIRTY-FIVE

The tigers moved with practised stealth. Within moments, they had encircled Alex, Leeuie and the alpacas. Any chance of escape was blocked. The creatures stared, unblinking, with eyes that were dark and hollow. Seeing, but not seeing. Black saliva dripped from their lips, and sharp shards of wood from Kiala's tree were stuck between their pointed teeth.

Icy dread seeped through Alex. This was a trap. And she had walked right into it.

A lazy wind eddied about the very top of the tree. The highest branches chafed against one another, creaking and scraping, creaking and scraping. The gust of air moved downward, scooping up fallen leaves and dirt, blowing them across the ground.

The wind picked up, stronger, a breathy whisper filling the forest. 'Attaaaaaack,' the wind called softly. 'Attack them.'

As one, the tigers crouched low. Teeth bared. Battle-ready.

The only hope they had of making it out of here alive

was to complete the binding ritual and sever the control Kiala had over the tigers. 'Can you hold them off while I do the ritual?' Alex asked in a low voice.

Moraika nodded, her eyes not moving from the tiger army. 'We're warriors. We were born for this.' Her woollen coat bristled. 'Form a barrier around Alex. Nothing gets past.'

The alpacas snapped into formation. Gone were the farmyard animals who lived for nothing but apples. In their place were wool-covered warriors, eyes hard, muscles taut. Alvaro clenched a large stick between his teeth. Lilly crouched low, eyes darting from one animal to the next, daring them to come any closer. Ollin scraped a groove in the dirt with his front foot, gnashing his teeth. 'We're ready for you,' he growled.

Leeuie followed their lead and unclipped his knife from his belt.

A tiger leaped at Alvaro. He swung the stick, catching the beast on the jaw and sending it flying. Three more charged, claws and teeth bared. Alvaro swiped them away.

Alex's hands shook. She grabbed the rock, bag of sand and white feather from her backpack.

Ollin reared up, kicking out with his front legs. He caught one tiger in the jaw, another in the soft flesh of its stomach. The tiger mewled in pain. Leeuie sliced at the air with his knife.

A fresh wave of leaves and twigs billowed around Alex.

She shielded her eyes, looking for Moraika. She needed some of the alpaca's blood. 'Moraika?' Three tigers snarled around Moraika's ankles. The alpaca booted them away before proffering a fresh wound on her leg to Alex.

Alex did not like the way Moraika's breath was coming out in rapid bursts. 'You okay?'

Moraika nodded, but her eyes were glassy and slightly unfocused. 'Hurry!'

Alex winced as she squeezed the edges of the cut. Blood dribbled out and pooled into her hand, warm and sticky, making her stomach turn.

A tiger leaped at Alex. Lilly clipped the creature's jaw with her foot, sending it tumbling across the clearing. 'Quick, Alex!'

Alex tried to focus. She had the ingredients. She knew the binding incantation. But there were so many other things she did not know. Was she meant to shout the incantation or whisper it? Touch the elements against the tree trunk? Bury them in the soil?

'Come on, Alex!' Leeuie said. He stabbed at the air, just managing to keep the tigers from pouncing on him with the threat of his knife.

Alex took a deep breath. *Please, please, please work.*

She pressed the white feather to the trunk of the tree and recited the first line of the binding incantation. The wind swirled faster. She lifted the volcanic rock, touched it to the trunk, and said the second line. The wind picked up even more, and a shiver travelled down Alex's spine. *It's working. I can feel it working!* She quickly brushed a small amount of black sand against the tree trunk and rubbed Moraika's blood along the pale, knotted wood as she recited the appropriate lines. The earth shuddered, as if trying to rid itself of some horrible sickness. Then, she spoke the final sentence.

'*With love I release you from your destiny!*'

Behind her, tigers snarled and spat. The alpacas and Leeuie grunted and shouted. Alex blinked. Surely the fighting would have stopped if the ritual had worked?

'What's going on?' Lilly shouted. Her voice was ragged and tight.

*It didn't work.* Alex stared at the elements in front of her, the awful realisation sinking in. 'It didn't work!'

'Then try again,' Lilly shouted. 'Fast!'

The fragments of light seeping through the forest were fading. Soon, it would be too dark to see anything. *Think,* Alex commanded herself. *What did I do wrong?*

Leeuie's frantic scream cut through her thoughts. 'Alex! Duck!'

A tiger was midair, leaping straight toward her. She flattened herself against the ground just as Leeuie slammed his body into the animal's gut. The boy and tiger careened sideways. The tiger hit the ground with a thump, rolling a few times. Leeuie plowed straight into the dirt and skidded along the ground, arms outstretched. Before he had come to a stop, the tiger was up, shaking itself and bounding towards him again.

Alex stood, grabbed the piece of volcanic rock and in two strides she was between Leeuie and the tiger. She brought the rock down on its skull. The animal stopped, swayed, and fell to the ground.

'Okay?' she called to Leeuie, who gave her a slightly bewildered nod.

She turned back to the tree, but her foot caught on a root and she stumbled forward, straight into the tree trunk. Pain seared through her palm as the bark cut into it. Alex snatched her hand away, but not before she saw a smear of blood smudged into the oozing black sap.

*Oh no, no, no, no!* Fear clutched at Alex. She forgot about everything going on around her as she frantically wiped her injured hand against her jeans, sap and blood smearing into the blue denim.

'Alex?' It was Leeuie.

She glanced up, and her heart stopped. She had been so distracted by what might happen if she'd got Kiala's poison on her, she hadn't noticed the stillness that had descended in the clearing. The tigers had ceased fighting and were standing, rigid and alert. Waiting.

Alex swallowed hard. *Waiting for what?*

Right at the top of the tree, there was a flicker of movement. The branches shook as a black shadow passed through them.

Alex's pulse drummed and her legs twitched, ready to run. She scooped the binding ritual elements into her backpack in case they had to move fast.

The shadow darted between the limbs, until it finally leaped from the lowest branch and landed on the ground with a soft, cushiony *whoosh*.

Alex gasped.

Standing before her was a young girl, eyes gleaming black and hard. 'At last, the weary years don't seem so long.' Her voice was soft and dangerous. Honey and arsenic. 'You have arrived.'

# Chapter Thirty-Six

The alpacas pressed together, a woolly knot next to Alex. Leeuie edged closer, too, his fingers white-knuckled around the hilt of his knife.

A cold shiver ran through Alex as she stared at the girl standing at the foot of the tree.

Kiala.

She was standing *right there* looking so much more than just awake. She looked alive. And very, *very* human.

Which meant Alex had failed. Spectacularly.

Kiala gingerly twisted her neck left and right, testing for stiffness. She lifted her arms, interlocking her fingers, stretching into the air. 'Thank you,' she said. 'I've been terribly uncomfortable for such a long time. But now …' She clasped her hands together at her chest, as though Alex was the new bike she'd wanted so desperately for her birthday.

'I knew one day you would come for me.'

Alex edged backwards. Kiala laughed, a sound of pure

childish delight. It wasn't the sort of sound Alex expected to hear from a thousand-year-old spirit capable of destroying everything around her in the blink of an eye.

In fact, nothing about Kiala was as she'd expected. For the most part, Kiala looked just like any other kid. Her knee-length white dress fluttered around her slight legs, and thick strands of long black hair framed her delicate features. In the dim light of the forest she didn't look menacing or ferocious. She looked fragile. Almost translucent.

But it was the eyes that gave away what she was. They were utterly fathomless, those eyes. Impossible to tell if they had witnessed everything — or nothing at all.

Kiala walked forward, tracing the path of a tree root with her steps, like it was a living balance beam and she wasn't allowed to touch the ground. Her steps were small, considered, and her eyes never left Alex as she came closer … closer … closer …

But then Moraika stepped in front of Alex, blocking Kiala's path.

'Stay away from her,' Moraika demanded.

Kiala's eyes flashed, angry and dangerous, and then a blast of air hurtled through the trees, exploding into Moraika. The alpaca was thrown onto her side, and the wind pushed her across the clearing.

Alex cried out and ran to Moraika, dropping to the dirt by her side. Moraika's face was contorted in pain, but she gave a small nod. *I'm okay.*

'That was a warning,' Kiala snarled. 'Next time I won't be so generous.'

Alex whirled to face Kiala, hands balled into fists. 'What do you want from us?'

Kiala's features transformed, and she was back to the smiling carefree girl again. In a few quick steps, she was standing right in front of Alex. Power radiated from her. Alex had to summon all her willpower not to turn and run. Not to show weakness.

Kiala leaned closer, whispering into Alex's ear. 'I want you to join me.' It was the same breathy voice that had whispered in Alex's ear the day she had arrived. It was the wind and the rain and the trees. There and not there at the same time.

And then, for a split second, the young girl ... flickered. For just the briefest moment, she disappeared.

Alex blinked. Was that her imagination? Behind her, the alpacas inhaled sharply. No, they saw it too.

Kiala was fading, becoming fuzzy and washed out at the edges, like a blurry photograph.

She suddenly backed away, moving closer to the tree trunk, like she was trying to hide what was happening.

Alex's heart skipped a beat. *She's still a spirit! She's not human yet!*

Alvaro leaned forward and whispered in Alex's ear, confirming her suspicions. 'I don't think she's achieved a corporeal form. What should we do?'

Alex's mind raced. What should they do? If Kiala wasn't human, then she didn't have her full power yet. And that meant maybe — just maybe — they could escape.

Alex made a decision. 'Run!'

Using her backpack as a weapon, Alex barrelled through the single line of tigers, knocking them sideways. Lilly, Ollin and Alvaro followed, kicking out left and right as they cantered. Moraika was still weak, but put on a burst of speed and, closely followed by Leeuie, raced after the others.

'Get on!' Alvaro cried, slowing just enough for Alex to throw herself onto his back and clutch his neck. Lilly performed an impressive mid-stride dip, and Leeuie jumped on.

Alex glanced behind her, expecting to see the tigers on her heels and Kiala with them, but the possessed animals had not budged and the young girl was standing at the edge of the clearing, her face a furious scowl. She raised her arms, and a wind started to blow. Alex didn't see Kiala's lips move, but words rang through the forest, carried on the wind, snaking between the trees.

'You have made the wrong choice.' The voice surrounded them. Engulfed them. 'And this time, I have the army. This time, I shall win!'

'Faster!' Alex yelled, leaning low against Alvaro's neck.

The swirling gale pressed at them from all directions. Alex's hair slapped at her face, biting into her skin. Alvaro strained against the wind, his steps faltering.

Then, as suddenly as it had started, the wind dropped and the forest settled back to stillness. They kept running, glancing back to see if there was anything following.

There wasn't.

'I think we can slow down!' Alex called after they'd thundered on for a while longer.

The alpacas were panting hard and grateful for the change of pace. Alex and Leeuie slid down to walk alongside them.

'Does anyone else think it's weird they aren't still chasing us?' Leeuie said, his voice shaky. 'Not that I'm complaining,' he added hurriedly.

'I think she's stuck there,' Alex said. She'd been replaying the whole thing over in her head. Everything Kiala had said, everything she'd done. 'Did you see how she was walking on the roots the whole time, making sure she was always touching some part of the tree? She can't totally seperate herself from it. She and the tree are still connected.'

Leeuie thought for a second, then nodded in agreement. He looked back over his shoulder. 'But she still could have sent the tigers or a firestorm after us.'

Alex knew he was right. But she didn't really want to think about it, because each time she did, she came to the same conclusion: that everything they'd done since entering the forest had been somehow playing directly into Kiala's grand plan.

# CHAPTER THIRTY–SEVEN

They walked on as dusk crept between the trees of the forest. Leeuie paused so he could consult his compass and make sure they were travelling in the right direction. The last thing they wanted to do was circle back to Kiala and her army.

'Hey, check it out!' Leeuie said, examining his palm closely then grinning. 'A splinter. A good one, too.'

A jolt of horror shot through Alex. 'Is it from Kiala's tree?' If Leeuie had got any of the sap on him, he could be poisoned. And worse, Kiala would be able to control him. 'Do you feel okay? Weird? Sick? Tired? Like someone's trying to take over your mind?'

Leeuie pressed experimentally at the splinter. 'I feel fine.'

From behind, Ollin huffed out a frustrated breath. 'Don't tell me he's going to turn into one of Kiala's lackeys. I'm too tired and hungry to run away from anything else today.'

Alex grabbed Leeuie's hand. The shard of wood was stuck deep into the fatty pad below his thumb, but she couldn't see any traces of black sap. Leeuie tried to pull away, but Alex wouldn't let him go. She peered into his face to see the colour of his eyes — to see if they had changed. But even in the low light she could tell they looked completely normal. Sandy brown shot with flecks of gold. Still …

'You should get the splinter out,' Alex said. 'Just in case.'

'No way.' Leeuie shook his head. 'I have to show Dad. This is the biggest one I've ever got.'

'But —'

'I *promise* I'm okay,' Leeuie said. 'Now can I have my hand back please?'

This time she let him tug his hand back and walk off. Alex hesitated for another moment, then followed. Very surreptitiously, she looked at her own hand. Back at the tree, she could have sworn she'd gotten the sap on her. She could have sworn it had mixed with her blood. But her hand looked and felt normal. A bit sore where she'd grazed it, but it hadn't swollen up like Mum's.

They hadn't gone more than a few steps when Moraika called from behind. 'Hey Alex?' The alpaca had stopped walking and was leaning against a tree. 'Can you ask Leeuie to slow down a bit? I can't walk as fast …'

Moraika trailed off as her eyes rolled back in her head. Her legs buckled under her and she collapsed onto the forest floor.

Alex screamed. She was the first to reach her, the first to see the deep gorge of red that ran the length of her neck. The first to see the dark blood pooling into her chocolate-coloured wool. Blood that now dripped freely onto the ground.

Alex tore off her jacket and pressed it to the alpaca's neck. Angry tears sprung to her eyes. How could she have been so stupid as not to notice that Moraika was hurt?

'We need to get her home. Now,' Alvaro said urgently. 'I can carry her. Ask Leeuie the quickest route.'

Alex translated as Leeuie wrenched off his own jacket to help stem the bleeding. 'My place is closest,' he said. 'But she'll need stitches. And fluids. She's lost a lot of blood. We'll have to get her to a vet.' He hesitated. 'And we'll have to come up with a story for what happened.'

'We don't have time to make up stories and wait for the vet!' Alex shouted. Moraika had been hurt — badly, badly hurt — by the one thing that could actually kill her. Kiala. 'She's dying!'

'Well,' Leeuie gulped. 'If we can get her back to my place ... I did see this documentary once about an animal hospital ...'

Alex was up before he had even finished the sentence. 'Let's go.'

Between them, they managed to hoist Moraika's listless body onto Alvaro, so she was slung over him like a sack of apples.

They walked fast, Leeuie leading the way, with Ollin and Lilly trotting next to him. Alex stayed beside Moraika, keeping pressure on the wound and stroking the alpaca's fur, whispering to her that they were nearly there, that everything was going to be okay.

An hour later, with night fully upon them, they emerged from the forest. Moraika's pulse was barely a flutter under Alex's fingers.

'Take her into the barn.' Leeuie pointed to a squat wooden structure to the left of his house. 'I'll sneak inside and find supplies.'

Alex flung the barn door open. Bales of hay were stacked against the far wall and Alex pulled one down to create a makeshift bed. Alvaro gently lowered Moraika onto it. The hay underneath her immediately turned red from the blood.

'Hang in there,' Alex whispered. Her own hands were stained rusty red, too. 'Just a bit longer.'

Compared to the forest, the barn was warm and dry, but Alex couldn't stop shivering. It was a tense ten minutes before Leeuie hurried back, his arms full.

'I had to sneak in through my bedroom window so my parents wouldn't see me,' he said, breathless, as he dumped everything on the floor — a bag of sugar, a shaker of salt, a large bottle that looked suspiciously like vodka and an industrial-size first-aid box. 'But they were already asleep. So we're safe.'

He picked up the bottle (which was, in fact, vodka) and emptied it over Moraika's wound and his own hands. 'I saw this on TV,' he explained. 'It's to disinfect the area.'

The group watched as Leeuie took a large curved needle

and thread from the first-aid box. His hand was shaking so badly he couldn't get the cotton through the eye.

'Here.' Alex took it from him. Her own hands weren't so steady either, but she managed to thread it on the third attempt. She gave him an encouraging smile as she handed it back. 'You can do this,' she said. *You have to do this,* she thought, her heart splintering at the prospect of losing Moraika.

Leeuie gulped. He tentatively inserted the needle into one side of the gaping cut.

'I think I'm going to be sick,' Ollin said, turning away.

Leeuie looked a bit like he was, too, but he took a deep breath and eased the needle out the other side, pulling the thread through the two sides of the wound.

The group sat in strained silence, watching as Leeuie made careful stitches down the length of Moraika's neck.

When he'd finished, he instructed Alex to fill a bucket with water. He tipped in the bag of sugar and the entire shaker of salt. 'For dehydration,' he explained.

He filled the empty vodka bottle and put it to Moraika's lips, but she was too far gone to swallow any of the liquid, and it just trickled onto the ground.

'Why won't she drink?' Lilly said, her voice small.

Alex put the question to Leeuie.

'I think she's in shock.' Leeuie sounded like he was trying not to cry. 'Her whole nervous system is shutting down. If we can just stabilise her and get her to take some fluids we might be in with a chance. But otherwise …' He bit his lip.

Alex sat up straight. 'Grandpa Jacob's medicine! It helped Mum when her body was in shock.'

Leeuie nodded. 'Anything's worth a try. I'll sneak inside and get the car keys.'

Alvaro unfurled his legs. 'Leeuie should stay. I'll take you.' He fixed his eyes on Ollin and Lilly. 'Moraika is in your care. Do not fall asleep on the job.'

'I couldn't sleep even if I wanted to,' Ollin said sadly.

# Chapter Thirty-eight

Alvaro cantered across the moonlit countryside to Grandpa Jacob's farm, with Alex clinging tightly around his neck. He came to a stop by the destroyed olive grove, panting hard, and Alex alighted from his back. The smell of charred wood hung bitter and heavy in the air.

Nerves kicked around Alex's stomach as she looked towards the bright, welcoming lights burning in the kitchen. She had momentarily forgotten about switching Grandpa Jacob's pills. He had wanted to bundle her and Mum off to a motel, then plough into the forest — fractured foot and all — to try and stop Kiala on his own. At the time, Alex had thought she would do a better job. At the time, she had been *positive* she could figure everything out.

And, sure, some of it she had. But not all of it. Not enough.

And now she had to tell him she'd tricked him for nothing. The binding spell hadn't worked. Moraika was dying. Mum wasn't getting better. Alex couldn't fathom how furious he was going to be, but she steeled herself. Moraika needed medicine. She was going to have to deal with whatever he threw at her.

'I'll wait in the barn,' Alvaro said quietly. 'Come and get me when you're ready to leave.'

***

The kitchen was empty when Alex let herself inside. She walked quietly down the hall, stopping in the doorway to Mum's room. Grandpa Jacob sat hunched over, his back to the door. He looked small, exhausted. In the bed, Mum was pale, her breathing laboured.

Alex bit her lip to stop from crying. It didn't take a genius to see Mum was getting worse. She was running out of time.

Sensing someone behind him, Grandpa Jacob spun around. His face contorted into a series of different expressions that Alex couldn't decipher. And then he heaved himself out of the chair and half-hopped, half-fell over the room, pulling Alex into a suffocating bear hug.

'You're okay,' he said over and over, his voice raw and relieved.

For a moment, Alex was too shocked to do anything, but then she wrapped her arms around his broad back and clung on tight.

Later, he sat at the kitchen table and listened as Alex gave him the abbreviated version of the events from the forest. The secret garden, the elements, the tigers. Kiala appearing from the tree. The binding ritual that hadn't worked.

When she told him about Moraika, he visibly paled and clutched at the edge of the table. Alex asked him about the medicine, if he thought it might work.

'It's worth a try,' he said. 'But I'll have to make some more. I gave Elina the last of it.'

Alex's heart sank. 'How long will that take?'

'A few hours.'

Alex just hoped Moraika could hang on that long.

Grandpa Jacob heaved himself from his chair and set about opening cupboards, collecting jars and bottles filled with some things Alex recognised and some she didn't. 'Why don't you get some sleep?' he said. 'I'll wake you when it's ready.'

Sleep. The thought of falling into a dreamless slumber was heavenly. But Alex knew there was no way she could. Or would. 'I'm not tired.'

He raised an eyebrow. 'I didn't think I was tired last night, so imagine my surprise when I had the best night's sleep I'd had in years.'

Alex cringed. 'About that. I'm really sorry.'

He regarded Alex for a long moment, not saying anything. Then he sighed. 'I'm the one who should be sorry.'

Alex frowned. 'You should?'

'I should have realised earlier how important you are.

That it was you all along.' He teetered on his moon boot, and flung it a disdainful look, muttering, 'And I certainly wouldn't be hobbling around with this cursed fractured foot if I'd known the truth about who you were.'

Alex blinked, then stared at her grandfather, incredulous. 'Are you saying you fractured your foot *on purpose* to try and get Wilfred to come and spend the summer here?'

His cheeks reddened and he looked away, suddenly very busy examining labels on jars.

Alex couldn't help it. She burst out laughing.

Grandpa Jacob gave her a sharp look. 'It's not exactly a laughing matter.'

'I know, I know …' She realised it wasn't *funny* funny, but she couldn't stop. The lengths that he had gone to seemed … well, it seemed like something just absurd and stupid enough for Alex to have tried herself. 'How did you do it?' she said between giggles.

He didn't say anything for a few moments, and then he mumbled, 'I dropped a crate of apples on it.'

This sent Alex into fresh peals of laughter.

His features softened. He started to chuckle and shook his head. 'Possibly the most stupid thing I've ever done,' he said. Then he looked down the hallway, towards the bedroom where Mum was sleeping. His shoulders slumped. 'Maybe the second most stupid.'

Alex took a moment to wipe away the tears of laughter. 'Why did you stop seeing Mum?'

He took a heavy breath and let it out, long and slow. 'I suppose it was after Wilfred was born. My whole life, I'd thought my first grandson was destined to stop Kiala. To save the world. So when he came along, nothing else mattered anymore. I knew what I had to do. While Rosa was alive it didn't matter so much. Rosa was the glue. She kept us together. Made sure we spoke on the phone. Made sure Elina came to visit. But after Rosa was gone ...' He shrugged helplessly. 'I lost track of time, I suppose. And then one day you wake up and realise you haven't spoken to your only daughter for ten years.' He hung his head, shaking it slowly. 'If I'd only known how wrong I was ...'

'If you'd known it was me all along then it would have been Mum and me invited here every summer?' Alex asked gently. 'You would have ignored Wilfred and Uncle Neil?'

Grandpa Jacob didn't answer for a long moment. 'I wish I could say no, but ...' He sighed again. 'I'm not proud of how I've behaved. It was idiotic. I was just so blinded by what I thought my purpose was that I forgot about what's actually important.' He huffed out a breath and looked again towards the spare room. 'All I can do is hope that she'll forgive me.'

'She will,' Alex said. And she knew she was right.

'Maybe.' Grandpa Jacob gave Alex a small, sad smile. 'But she needs to wake up first.'

# CHAPTER THIRTY-NINE

'Tell me about the binding ritual,' Grandpa Jacob said, adding oil gradually to a powder of crushed herbs and leaves. 'About why it didn't work.'

Alex had been over it again and again in her head, and still had no idea why it hadn't worked. Had she said the incantation wrong? Did she use too much, or too little, of each element? Were the elements even correct? There were too many moving parts, too many unknowns.

She explained about the incantation and how each line of it described what the elements were. A feather from the white eagle, a volcanic rock, sand from beneath the waterfall, Moraika's blood.

Grandpa Jacob's eyebrows shot up. 'Moraika's blood?'

Alex nodded. 'The blood of a hero.'

'But …' He frowned. 'How does that work if she isn't in her body anymore? The blood running through her isn't hers.'

Alex opened her mouth to answer, then shut it again. His words sunk in and Alex realised with dismay that he was right. The actual, physical blood running through Moraika's current body wasn't hers. It hadn't been hers since the warriors had magically made their spirits immortal and transferred them to animal bodies.

Alex dropped her head into her hands and groaned loudly. No wonder the binding ritual hadn't worked!

'I can't do the ritual if I can't get Moraika's blood,' she said, her voice muffled.

'Hold up,' Grandpa Jacob said. He stopped what he was doing. 'You can. Her blood isn't running through her anymore ... but it is running through you.'

Alex lifted her head. She stared at him.

'You're descended from Moraika.' He was talking fast now, excited. 'You *literally* have her blood. The prophecy even says it. *The power returns with the Fortieth Sun, it's thanks to their blood that the task can be done*! Their blood. Your blood!'

'You said that wasn't to do with actual blood,' Alex reminded him.

Grandpa Jacob snorted. 'And I've been so right about everything else, haven't I?'

Alex rolled the idea around in her head. The blood of the hero. The blood passed down through generations until it reached the fortieth descendant. The blood that could put Kiala back to sleep. Her blood.

Then, Alex froze. 'It's my blood.'

'That's what I'm saying.' Grandpa Jacob grinned. 'That's why the ritual didn't work!'

Alex shook her head. She knew he was right about that, but she had just remembered something else. Well, really three something elses.

First, when she had arrived at the farm and got the splinter by the front gate. A drop of her blood had stained the fence post and immediately afterwards the wind had rushed from the forest and whispered in her ear. *Ready or not, here I come.* That was the moment Kiala had woken up.

Second, unloading the apple crates she'd got another splinter. Leeuie had removed it, and although it hadn't hurt, there had been some blood. She'd sucked it away, but then spat it onto the ground. Soon after that, Kiala had sent the firestorm that decimated the olive grove.

And third, when she was in the forest by Kiala's tree she had fallen over and grazed her hand on one of the roots. The ghostly vision of Kiala had appeared straight after. Alex's blood had been spilled again, and Kiala had become strong enough to show herself outside the tree.

Alex stood up so fast her chair toppled over. *This is all my fault …*

'What?' Grandpa Jacob stared at her, concerned. 'What is it?'

She paced to the sink, the fridge, then back to the table, her voice hoarse as she told Grandpa Jacob everything she'd realised.

'Alex, Alex!' Grandpa Jacob stopped her in her tracks by putting his hands on her shoulders. He bent down so he was looking into her ashen face. 'You did nothing wrong.'

'I've done everything wrong!' Alex shouted, tears springing to her eyes. 'I woke her up just by getting a stupid splinter from a fence post. She got stronger because I hurt my thumb. I scraped my hand in the forest and it meant she could get out of the tree. Every time I hurt myself she gets stronger! It's my fault she woke up ten years early!'

'Yes, but none of us knew this could happen.' He gently manoeuvred Alex to a chair and sat her down. 'And you're forgetting the most important point. It's *your blood* that will put her back to sleep. You are the key to restoring balance.'

'But none of this would be happening if I hadn't started it!' Alex shouted.

'It was an accident.' He shrugged. 'A mistake. It's happened. And all we can do is try to put it right.' He hesitated. 'Actually, I think you should consider yourself rather lucky.'

Alex felt the exact opposite of lucky. 'Why?'

'Because unlike so many mistakes from the past that we don't know how to fix, you know why the ritual failed. And you know what to do to fix it.'

Alex nodded. *Yes*, she thought slowly. *I do know that. And Kiala doesn't know I know.*

'I have to go back in,' she said. 'I have to go back to the forest right now.'

This time, Grandpa Jacob didn't argue with her.

# CHAPTER FORTY

Grandpa Jacob added the final ingredient to the medicine just as the shrill sound of the birds' dawn chorus sounded outside. He poured the purple liquid into two bottles. He was about to hand one to Alex, but hesitated.

'Will you take the others back into the forest with you?' he asked.

Alex didn't respond immediately. She had everything she needed to complete the ritual and didn't want to put the others in more danger than she already had. On top of that, if she was going to have any chance of performing the ritual before Kiala could mobilise her tiger army, she needed absolute stealth — to get to Kiala unnoticed.

'I'm going on my own,' she eventually said. 'I *have* to go on my own.'

He closed his eyes. 'Okay,' he said, his voice barely a whisper.

\*\*\*

At the back door, Grandpa Jacob cleared his throat. 'Before you leave …' He pulled something from his pocket. 'I made this for Rosa. I want you to have it.'

It was a necklace, long and elegant. The centrepiece was a smooth oval stone — shiny and black — shaped like an olive. On either side were delicate, translucent beads in an assortment of colours and sizes. A fragile shape was suspended inside each one. Alex squinted closer. 'Are they tiny flowers?'

Grandpa Jacob smiled. 'They're all from our farm. I pressed them in resin myself. When Rosa got too sick to go outside, I brought the outside to her.' He touched the shiny black stone in the middle. 'This stone, too. She said it gave her strength.' His voice cracked. 'Made her feel grounded.'

Alex didn't know what to say. No one had ever given her anything so precious before.

Grandpa Jacob misread her silence. His face flushed and he went to take the necklace back. 'It's silly. You don't want it.'

'No, I do!' Alex slipped it over her head. It was the perfect length, the perfect weight, the perfect balance of colours. 'It's beautiful,' she said, cupping the centre stone in her palm. 'It's my good luck charm.'

\*\*\*

Soft pink light was just starting to steal around the edges of the horizon as Alex tied the bottle of medicine around Alvaro's neck and watched him canter off towards Leeuie's house.

She'd known Alvaro wouldn't let her go into the forest alone, so she'd told him she was going to stay at the farmhouse and sleep for a few hours. He'd given her a long, hard look, but Alex didn't flinch. Didn't even blink.

After the alpaca disappeared, Alex leaned down to retrieve her backpack from where she'd hidden it behind the olive grove fence.

She was just about to heave it onto her shoulder when she stopped. She peered down. Her heart skipped a beat. Right next to the fence was an olive sapling. She crouched down, running her fingers gently over the top of the tree. The tiny grey-green leaves were waxy and firm. Robust. Alex smiled. One of the olive trees had survived! It wasn't much, given the devastation Kiala had inflicted, but it was something.

Remembering how sick Kiala's tree in the forest had looked, Alex eased the olive sapling from the ground. That big old tree wasn't going to last another thousand years with Kiala imprisoned in it. But this lithe young sapling just might.

She tucked the tiny tree into the inside pocket of her jacket, then looked towards the forest. A seed of hope took root inside her. Kiala was not going to take everything from them. Alex wouldn't let her.

# CHAPTER FORTY-ONE

As Alex made her way quietly through the forest, she wondered if Alvaro had made it back to Leeuie's farm with the medicine yet. She desperately wished she could be there when (it had to be *when*, there was no *if* about it) Moraika woke up. She imagined Leeuie untying the bottle from Alvaro (probably saying something about how Alex should have used this or that knot, rather than the haphazard attachment she did use), then feeding it to Moraika. Alex pictured the alpaca waking suddenly and trying to spit the foul taste from her mouth. The others would cry and hug — did alpacas hug? — and then fall into a happy but exhausted sleep, only getting up again when Alex returned, triumphant.

She clung to these thoughts, wrapping them around herself as she made her way, step by silent step, towards Kiala's tree.

Up ahead, a branch snapped. Alex stopped. She listened. She didn't even dare breathe. Her eyes darted left and right. There was nothing but trees, trees and more trees.

She took a shaky breath and kept walking, gladly embracing the knowledge that, after this was all over, she would *never* have to walk through this creepy forest again. Because this ended one of two ways: Alex succeeded and Kiala was gone forever, or she failed and they all died.

*I just need to be invisible. I just need to get to the tree. I just need to do the ritual.*

But that wasn't to be.

After only a few more steps, the leaves around her rustled, and scores of beady black eyes peered through the gloom. Two, then six, then thirty.

Alex's heart plummeted to her shoes, straight through them, and all the way to the middle of the earth.

The tigers. They had found her.

One by one, they stepped forward, appearing from between the trees like striped ghosts.

Alex snatched a stick from the ground. 'Get away from me!' She swung the stick. It swished harmlessly through the air. 'Go on! Get lost!'

The tigers didn't attack. They didn't even growl. Instead, they marched forward and surrounded Alex. She felt a nudge on the back of her knees and stumbled forward. The tigers moved with her, forcing her to walk. And then she understood. She was their prisoner and they were taking her to Kiala.

As she walked, Alex ran through every possible scenario in which she didn't end up dead. There were depressingly few. She kicked herself for not packing a dozen large, juicy steaks laced with Grandpa Jacob's sleeping pills to feed to the tigers … or Grandpa Jacob's rifle … or an invisibility cloak, a rocket-launcher, a hovercraft …

By the time they reached the clearing where Kiala's tree stood, the sky was properly light. The tigers herded Alex in, then formed a circle around the space, each one standing a few feet away from its neighbour, eyes trained forward.

Alex glanced around, looking for Kiala. Her eyes paused on the tree. It looked smaller than last time. No, not smaller exactly, but as though it didn't have the strength to hold itself up anymore.

The tigers stepped forward, forcing Alex closer to the tree. And then she saw Kiala. The young girl sat on the lowest branch, her bare feet swinging back and forth. She looked different, too. Smudgy and insignificant. A washed-out memory of the girl Alex had seen before.

Kiala lifted a translucent arm, waving it over the circle of tigers. 'Sit,' she commanded.

As one, the tigers sat. About half of them kept moving slightly — tails swiping slowly against the dirt, ears twitching — but the other half became absolutely still. Frozen.

Alex allowed the tiniest flicker of hope to flare inside her. Being outside of the tree must be taking its toll on Kiala. Her power had to be draining more quickly because she had to draw energy not only to control the tigers, but to enable her spirit to move about. She was a battery hooked up to too many devices.

Kiala didn't bother with pleasantries this time. She pointed to the backpack slung over Alex's shoulders. 'Bring that here.'

Alex hesitated. She needed to stall for time. Figure out a way to drain Kiala's power even further so that she might have a chance of doing the binding ritual.

But Kiala was not in the mood for Alex's games. She snapped her fingers. One of the tigers broke rank and walked toward Alex. The creature snarled, displaying its incredible jaw. Teeth sharp as daggers dripped with black poisonous saliva and small bits of bark were stuck between its teeth.

'Your bag,' Kiala repeated, her voice ice cold.

The final word was punctuated by another growl from the tiger. Alex slipped off the backpack. The tiger walked back to rejoin the ranks.

'Good girl,' Kiala said.

Alex couldn't tell if Kiala was talking to her or the tiger.

'What have you done to them?' Alex asked, nodding toward the tigers. Maybe if she could keep Kiala talking it would tire her out?

'We have a mutual understanding,' Kiala said. 'They do me little favours now and again, and I keep them alive.'

'Everyone thinks Tasmanian tigers are extinct.' Alex swallowed, trying to keep her voice even and calm. 'Why hasn't anyone seen them until now?'

Kiala smiled thinly. 'Never reveal an advantage until

you're going to use it. I learned that from your dear ancestor. Before she … ruined me.' Kiala brought a finger to her pale throat and, very slowly, made a slicing motion across it. Her pale skin shimmered and wavered and she laughed, a high, maniacal sound. 'How is Moraika, by the way? Dead yet?'

Fury built inside Alex. But she couldn't lose her cool. Not yet. Not until she had a plan. 'She's fine,' Alex said and desperately hoped it was true.

Kiala shrugged. She slid down from the tree, landing light as a spider onto a tree root that snaked above the surface of the ground. 'And your mother?' The spirit's voice was saccharine laced with ice. 'How is she?'

It was all Alex could do not to run at the spirit and tackle her to the ground. 'You're not getting my mum!'

Kiala smirked at Alex's outburst. 'No?'

'Grandpa Jacob's got this medicine,' Alex said, words tumbling out faster and faster, 'and it's strong enough to stop her doing what you say, and he'll keep making it forever and ever, so it doesn't matter what you do to me, you're never going to be able to put your stupid spirit in Mum's body!'

Kiala stared at Alex incredulously, then tipped her head back and laughed. 'Put my spirit in her body? What an absurd notion. She cannot contain me. I need someone strong but balanced. I need you.'

'Me?' Alex frowned. 'How can I …' She trailed off as she realised the enormity of what Kiala had just said. She recalled getting the black sap on her hand last time she was here. How nothing had happened to her. Being the Fortieth Sun — having the blood of the Chodzanar warriors flowing through her — meant she was the *only* one who could withstand Kiala's power. She was the only one who could balance it out.

Around her, the world slowed. Everything was suddenly crystal clear. Alex stared at her backpack, which was resting by Kiala's feet. Inside the bag was everything needed to complete the binding ritual. And now Alex was here, too, alone. Her hunch from earlier about Kiala needing a new body had been right. Kiala was going to perform the binding ritual and put her spirit into Alex's body.

Kiala had let Alex, Leeuie and the alpacas pass through the forest and into the secret garden unharmed because she needed Alex to collect the elements for her. The tigers had herded them here as soon as Alex had collected everything. This whole time, they had been doing exactly what Kiala wanted. *Stupid, stupid, stupid!*

'Ahhh,' Kiala said softly. 'Finally, you're beginning to understand.' Without taking her eyes from Alex's face, she reached out to touch the backpack. Her hand went straight through it.

Alex's stomach flipped. Kiala couldn't touch anything. She couldn't hold anything. Which meant she couldn't perform the binding ritual herself. Which meant … 'You were going to use Mum to perform the binding ritual,' Alex said, her voice hoarse. 'You were going to get her to kill me.'

'Not kill. Liberate.'

Queasiness engulfed Alex. But then a small voice in the back of her mind whispered, *Don't get distracted. Kiala can't perform the ritual. Grandpa Jacob's just given Mum more medicine. There's still a chance …*

Alex only needed a minute. One single minute and she could do the ritual. One single minute and she could put everything right.

'Now, now,' Kiala said. She waggled a pale finger. 'Don't get any ideas. Your mother might be unavailable to me, but I always have a backup plan. Always.' She paused and clasped her hands together, peering around the huge trunk of her tree. 'Don't be shy. You can come out now and say hello to Alexandra.'

With slow, careful steps, a figure emerged from behind the tree. 'Hello Alex.'

# CHAPTER FORTY-TWO

Alex felt like the forest floor had dropped out from beneath her feet.

Leeuie.

Kiala had Leeuie. Alex kicked herself for believing him when he said the splinter wasn't from Kiala's tree. For letting herself think he was fine. For getting him involved in the first place.

Leeuie walked toward Alex, his gait slow and face blank. His normally sandy-coloured eyes were huge and black.

Alex pleaded with Kiala. 'He's got nothing to do with this. Please don't hurt him.'

'What a peculiar thing for you to be concerned with at the moment,' Kiala said. She turned to Leeuie. 'Empty her bag.'

Alex blocked his path. 'No, Leeuie, listen to me —'

He hissed at Alex, and slapped her out of the way. She stumbled sideways, her cheek stinging.

Leeuie unzipped her backpack and started pulling the

contents out. He lined up the elements for the binding ritual in a neat row at the base of the tree. Kiala crouched next to them, her face alight with joy. Although she couldn't hold or touch them, the elements seemed to sense her presence. The feather fluttered. The black sand rippled, fighting against the plastic that contained it. The volcanic rock glowed a deep, dark red.

The only thing missing for the ritual to be completed was Alex's blood.

'Tie her up,' Kiala demanded.

Leeuie grabbed Alex. She kicked and punched and screamed at him to stop, but her shouts and blows didn't even register. He was strong. Much stronger than her. Much stronger than he should have been.

He threw her hard against the trunk and she gasped, winded. Rope scratched at her ankles as Leeuie tied them tight together. She pounded blows on his back, trying to break free. He hissed again and shoved her, hard. She fell sideways, landing heavily on the ground. Leeuie rammed her back up against the tree, looping the rope around her wrists and tying it in a simple knot.

'That'll do,' Kiala said, impatient. 'She's not going anywhere.'

Leeuie unclipped the large hunting knife from his belt and shook it free from its sheath. The blade glinted steely grey.

Panic flared and Alex tried to scramble away, but with

her wrists and ankles bound she barely got a few inches before Leeuie pushed her back.

'If you don't struggle,' Kiala said, her voice soft and dangerous, 'it won't hurt as much.'

'Please Leeuie,' Alex croaked. 'Please don't do this.'

He lifted the knife, and Alex watched in horror as the blade came down ... and went straight into the trunk of the tree.

Alex's heart hammered against her ribs. Had he missed?

Black sap oozed around the blade, and Leeuie collected some of the sticky mess in his hand. With his other hand, he roughly grabbed Alex's chin and tilted her head back, prying her mouth open.

No, he hadn't missed. Kiala wanted her to eat the poisonous sap.

She tried to shake him off, tried to keep her lips tightly pressed together, but Leeuie was too strong. Alex choked as he pushed some of the sap into her mouth, then forced her to swallow.

The foul substance burned her throat and hit her stomach like lead. The sap felt like it was tearing her apart from the inside out. She was boiling hot, then icy cold, and everything around her swam in and out of focus. She tried to cling to reality, but it seemed to fade further and further away.

And then Alex wasn't in the forest anymore.

She was ... Where was she?

A grassy field, surrounded by mountains. Two little girls ran and played, happy and laughing, totally unaware that Alex was there watching them. They were identical, right down to the dimples in their cheeks and the white tunics they wore.

Alex knew who they were. Kiala and Resila.

One girl picked a flower and it wilted in her hands. The other breathed life back into it.

'Magic,' said Resila.

Kiala shook her head. 'Power.'

The image faded, and Alex saw the same two girls, older now, arguing. She was so close to them, she could have reached out and touched them, but they paid no attention to her. *I'm not really here*, Alex thought. *This is a memory. Kiala's memory.*

'We could be gods,' Kiala was shouting at her sister. 'More than gods. We could have everything!'

Resila kept her voice low and calm. 'But what we have is enough.'

Kiala scowled. 'You're a fool if you think that.'

The picture shifted again. There was Kiala, older again, eyes wild, face covered in dirt and dust and blood. Resila was kneeling in front of her.

'Please stop,' Resila begged, clutching at the hem of her sister's dress.

'Not until you join me!' Kiala said.

'I can't do that.'

'Can't or won't?' Kiala snarled.

Resila hesitated for a moment. 'Won't.'

In a blind rage, Kiala shook her sister free, pushed her away. Resila flew through the air, landing hard on the ground. Too hard.

'Get up!' Kiala growled, when her sister didn't move. 'Get up and fight.'

But Resila didn't. She lay very still.

'Resila?' Kiala seemed to wilt. She collapsed on the ground next to her sister. 'Get up,' she whispered, a tear slipping down her face. 'Please get up.'

Nearby, there was shouting and four people approached at speed. Kiala stumbled to her feet, then turned and fled.

The scene shifted once more, and Alex was in a temple. Kiala was there, her tears gone, her face hard. At the sound of someone approaching she raised her arms, ready to fight.

'Hello, sister,' Resila said.

Kiala dropped her hands. 'You're ... you're alive?'

Before Resila could answer, four people sprang out of hiding. Alex knew them immediately. Moraika, Alvaro, Lilly and Ollin in their human forms. The warriors.

They grabbed Kiala's arms and legs and threw her onto the large stone table where they quickly fastened heavy chains around her wrists and ankles. The metal was fortified with magic, and although Kiala strained against them, the chains held fast, chafing her skin red and raw. 'Help me!' she cried. 'Sister, help me!'

But Resila didn't. She stepped back, turning her head away.

Confusion flickered across Kiala's face, and then her eyes narrowed. 'You traitor!' she said. 'Because of you they will kill me.'

'You killed her first,' Ollin said. 'Or, you tried to.'

'I didn't!' Kiala spat. She turned to her sister. 'It was an accident. I would never hurt you, sister. Not on purpose. You know that!'

Resila couldn't look her in the eye. 'I told you to stop,' she said. 'I begged you.'

'And now I'm begging you!' Kiala strained against the chains again. 'Stop this before anyone else gets hurt!'

Resila closed her eyes, her face a picture of misery and pain.

Kiala turned her wrath on the warriors. 'I suppose you think you're clever,' she said. 'Turning my sister against me, like this. But you'll never stop me. Nothing can stop me!'

The warriors ignored her and focused instead on three clay pots that were lined up on the table. Ollin reached inside and extracted a white feather.

*They're doing the binding ritual!* Alex realised.

Ollin touched the feather to Kiala's forehead, speaking his line of the incantation.

Kiala paled. 'No, no, no! Sister! You can't let them do this!'

Resila didn't open her eyes. 'What choice have you left us?'

'I'll stop,' Kiala said, pleading. 'I promise I'll stop.'

Resila's eyes flew open. She looked to the warriors, hopeful.

'She's lying,' said Alvaro. 'Don't listen to her.'

Kiala looked beseechingly at her sister. 'I'm the only one you should listen to!'

Lilly was next, with the black stone, then Alvaro with the sand.

'You think these people will leave you alone once I'm gone?' Kiala said. 'They won't. They're just as scared of you as they are of me. They don't understand us.'

'Don't *listen* to her!' Lilly said.

'I'm your family,' Kiala cajoled. 'Your *twin*. Without me, you're nothing.' Her voice cracked. 'Without you, I'm nothing.'

Resila's hands flew to her mouth as she let out a sob.

Moraika took a dagger from her belt and sliced her own hand. She dribbled blood onto Kiala's forehead, and the girl screamed as though it burned.

Moraika then lifted the dagger high into the air. Resila stepped towards the table, eyes wide and uncertain. 'Wait!'

Moraika hesitated. She turned to Resila. 'You must bless this binding ritual with your magic,' she said. 'If you do not, it will never hold.'

'I don't know if I can,' Resila said.

'You must decide,' Moraika said, her voice firm and even. 'Is the blood of one worth more than the blood of an empire?'

'Tell them it is!' Kiala cried. There were real tears now. Real fear in her eyes. Real sadness.

'Is the blood of one worth more than the blood of an empire?' Moraika repeated, urgent now, her hand starting to shake.

Resila was on the edge. She bit her lip, looking from the knife to her sister and back again. 'I ... I don't know.'

'Decide!'

And then Resila shook her head and turned away.

Moraika chanted the final words of the incantation, then the knife plunged down.

# CHAPTER FORTY-THREE

Alex gasped, and she was back to reality. A reality where the side of her face was smushed against the forest floor from where she'd fallen onto her side, and Kiala was leaning down, peering closely at her.

'Oh good,' Kiala said. 'You're not dead.'

Alex scrambled to sit up. She felt dazed and had the most horrific taste in her mouth, but at least she wasn't burning from the inside out anymore.

Kiala smirked. 'I had to make sure you were able to withstand my power. I couldn't have you dying on me once I'd taken over your body. Then where would I be?' She moved so she was sitting cross-legged on the ground near Alex, and then rested her slender back against the trunk of the tree. Almost immediately, half of her disappeared into the mottled grey-brown of the bark and the tree seemed to sigh.

Underneath her, Alex could feel the roots breathe with renewed energy. Kiala in the tree was powerful but trapped. Kiala out of the tree was weak but free. The spirit both drew on and fed into the power of her prison.

'Let's begin,' Kiala said, and her voice seemed to come from everywhere.

Alex needed more time. She needed to get Kiala away from the tree. To weaken her. 'No, wait!' she said. 'Your sister. I know about her.'

Kiala spun to face her, moving away from the tree. 'What do you know of my *sister*?'

'That you didn't kill her,' Alex said.

'More fool me,' Kiala spat. 'She was a traitor!'

Alex remembered what Moraika had asked Resila. *Is the blood of one worth more than the blood of an empire?* She remembered how the girl had hesitated.

'She didn't want to do it,' Alex said.

A flicker of sadness momentarily creased Kiala's features. But then vengeance was back.

'I'm done with talking,' Kiala said. 'Shut her up and begin.'

Leeuie pressed his forearm across Alex's collarbone, pinning her against the tree. Bark jabbed painfully into her spine. Breathing was difficult. Talking was impossible.

Leeuie picked up the white feather and brushed it to Alex's forehead as Kiala spoke the words, her lilting voice echoing through the forest. '*As pure as light I soar and swoop.*'

Alex thought desperately. She struggled against Leeuie's arm but he held her fast and touched the rock to her forehead. The stone was hot, like it was on fire from the inside. Kiala spoke the accompanying words. Then he sprinkled sand as Kiala recited the incantation.

All that was left now was Alex's blood.

She struggled and fought, shouting and crying, not thinking of anything past the immediate fact she had to get free right now. But she had nothing. And before she knew it, Leeuie had picked up the knife, flicked his wrist, and Alex felt a sharp sting on her arm. It was a tiny nick, less than a centimetre, but blood pooled from it. Leeuie swiped his thumb across it and smeared blood across her forehead.

The incantation flowed out of Kiala like a song. '*An elixir of life that only the hero can bring forth.*'

And then Leeuie lifted the knife high into the air. This time, he wasn't aiming for the tree.

A sob welled inside Alex. All her panic and fury slipped away. There wasn't any point fighting anymore. She was out of options.

Alex squeezed her eyes shut, unable to watch anymore. *I'm so sorry, Mum*, she thought. *I'm so sorry, Grandpa Jacob.*

All she could do now was wait for Kiala to say the final words of the incantation. *With love I release you from your destiny.* And for the knife to pierce her throat.

# Chapter Forty-four

But the final words never came, and the knife never struck.
Instead, thunderous noise erupted all around Alex. The
ground shook. There was a sickening thud and Leeuie's arm
was gone. Alex's eyes flew open.

There was Ollin.

And Lilly.

And Alvaro.

And … 'Moraika!' Alex cried. 'You're okay!'

Kiala leaped up, screaming at the tigers. 'Don't just sit
there! Stop them!'

The alpacas formed a tight protective group around Alex
as Moraika bit at the rope binding her wrists. The alpaca was
breathing hard and seemed a bit unsteady on her feet, but
she was very much alive.

'You shouldn't be here, you should be resting!' Alex said,
even though she had never been as happy to see anyone — or
any alpaca — in her entire life.

'You think we'd let you come out here alone?' Moraika

said around a mouthful of rope.

Alex shook her wrists free and looked around for Leeuie. She gasped when she saw his motionless body sprawled at the edge of the clearing. 'He's not …'

'Just unconscious,' Alvaro called, kicking out at a tiger. 'I may have head-butted him a little hard.'

The tigers growled and scratched at the alpacas, but their ferocity was muted. 'It's like they're not really trying,' Ollin said, using a front leg to box a tiger square in the jaw.

'Kiala's weak, so the tigers are weak.' Alex tugged at the rope around her ankles, freeing them. 'If you can hold them off for a bit longer I can do the ritual. I know what I did wrong last time.'

Kiala's voice sliced through the clearing. 'Why do you insist on fighting me? You know you can never win.'

'You sure about that?' Ollin called, cocky as he took out three tigers at once. 'Ha! Take that! And that!'

Kiala threw her head back and laughed. Lightning crackled overhead. 'You were foolish when you were human, and I see you've not improved with your change.'

She placed her hand against the tree. Immediately, the tigers stopped what they were doing and became stony statues once again.

The alpacas stopped, too. 'What are they doing?' Lilly asked, her voice wary, her gaze flicking from one motionless tiger to the next.

Kiala closed her eyes, and her fingertips morphed into

the bark. Her image flickered. Power pulsed through the air.

'Do the ritual,' Moraika said, and there was an urgency in her voice that Alex hadn't heard before. 'Right now!'

With her heart beating way too fast, Alex sank onto the ground in front of the elements. *This had better work.*

Kiala withdrew her hand from the tree, and the world exploded.

The tigers threw themselves at the alpacas, scratching, biting, snarling. Lilly screamed as a tiger raked its claws through the flesh of her leg. Blood stained her caramel coat. Ollin balanced on his front legs and kicked hard at the tiger, sending it flying. 'Hurry, Alex!'

Alex slapped the feather against the tree, then threw the rock, shouting the two lines of the incantation as quickly as she could. She tried to block out the alpacas' gasps and cries as the tigers attacked, unrelenting, too strong. This was not a fair fight.

Kiala spoke over the noise, her words tantalising and slow, a complete contrast to the ferocious battle. 'You'll never beat me.'

'Don't listen to her!' Alvaro cried.

Kiala smiled, cruel and bitter. And then the tigers were upon Alvaro, all teeth and claws and poison, pulling him to the ground.

Alex cried out. 'Alvaro! No!'

'If you give up now, I will let them all live!' Kiala crowed. 'You have my word.'

Alex hesitated. Kiala was lying. Of course she was lying. But ... what if she wasn't? Alex's mind skipped back once more to the question that Moraika had asked Resila during the original binding ritual. *Is the blood of one worth more than the blood of an empire?* Was Alex's life more important than the alpacas, Mum, Grandpa Jacob, Leeuie? Than everyone else in the world? If there was even the slightest chance Kiala was telling the truth, wasn't it worth sacrificing herself?

'It's never going to work,' Kiala cried.

'Don't give up!' Moraika pleaded. 'The ritual *will* work.'

Alex nodded. Yes. She knew last time she had the wrong blood. This time, it was going to work. It had to work.

She threw a pinch of sand against the tree, then snatched Leeuie's knife from the ground and nicked her finger. She smeared a sticky smudge of the blood along the bark, shouting the lines of the incantation.

Thunder rumbled overhead and wind careened through the clearing, drowning out the sounds of the battle.

Filled with hate for the spirit who was attacking her friends, who had tried to kill Mum, Alex snatched Leeuie's knife from the ground and plunged the blade into the tree, spitting out the final words of the incantation. '*With love I release you from your destiny*!'

She couldn't see Kiala as she wrestled the small olive sapling from the inside pocket of her coat and gripped it tight, waiting, waiting.

*Please, please, please …*

A fork of lightning struck a tree nearby and a large limb broke off, crashing to the ground. The roots of the huge olive tree undulated, making the earth tremble.

Kiala's laughter swirled through the forest. Alex lost her balance and dropped the olive sapling.

'You've gotta be kidding me!' Alex shouted into the wind. The binding spell hadn't worked. Again!

A tiger leaped across the clearing, slamming into Moraika and knocking her over. The tiger snarled, its gaze trained on the bloody mess of the alpaca's neck.

Alex yelled at the creature. She grabbed the volcanic rock and pitched it at the tiger's head. At the same time, Ollin leaped through the air and slammed against the tiger. The creature rolled across the ground. The black rock sailed harmlessly through the air, tumbling outside the edge of the clearing and into the forest. Ollin skidded and fell. He and Moraika were immediately surrounded by tigers, poised to strike.

Alex screamed. 'No! Please, no!'

'Stop!' Kiala lifted her arms and the battle stilled. She prowled toward Alex, slow, a silken predator, her face a triumphant smile. 'You have one last chance. Do what I ask, or you can watch them all die.'

Alex took in the scene before her. The alpacas were trapped. The tigers prowled around them, victorious.

*Is the blood of one worth more than the blood of an empire?*

Alex's body was suddenly too heavy, too sore. The binding ritual didn't work and she had no idea why. She had lost.

'I'll do what you want,' she said softly. 'Let them go.'

# Chapter Forty-Five

Kiala clapped her hands, delighted. The alpacas gasped and looked at one another.

'And you have to make Mum and Leeuie better, and leave Grandpa Jacob alone,' Alex demanded.

Kiala cocked an eyebrow. 'You hardly seem to be in a position to bargain.'

'I don't see anyone else here who can perform the binding ritual for you,' Alex retorted.

Kiala actually looked impressed. 'Alright. You perform the binding ritual to put my spirit into your body, and I will spare them all.' Her mouth twisted into a strange little smile. 'In fact, I will do more than that. I will save those you love, and make those you don't, pay.'

A chill travelled the length of Alex's spine. 'What's that supposed to mean?'

Kiala leaned close. 'It means I will make sure your sister atones for her sins.'

Alex could not keep the shock off her face. How did

Kiala know about Dad's new kid?

'Oh, I have eyes and ears everywhere,' Kiala said, waving away Alex's unspoken question. 'And I know how it feels to be forgotten. To be unloved. To be second-best. Just like you are to her. You have my word that I will make her suffer for what she has done. This is my gift to you.'

A sensation welled inside Alex that she could not quite describe, but it made her feel very, very small and very, *very* stupid. Luciana hadn't done anything. She was just a baby! She wasn't responsible for Alex having a fight with her dad. No, that was all on Alex. 'Leave my sister out of this.'

A flicker of uncertainty passed across Kiala's face, but then the glassy jet-black eyes and stony expression were back. 'There comes the day that you need to make a choice,' Kiala spat. 'You can let them destroy you, or you can destroy them.'

'That's just really …' Alex was about to say 'stupid' but she stopped herself. A pang of — what was that? Sorrow? — tugged somewhere inside her. It wasn't stupid. It was sad. Unbearably sad.

All of a sudden, Alex felt an overwhelming sense of pity for the girl standing before her. Kiala had not chosen her gift — her curse — but she had let it whisper jealousy and heartache and war in her ears. She had let it push away everyone who loved her. And then Kiala had been put to death by her own sister. Her own family.

*With love I release you from your destiny …*

Alex sucked in a sharp breath. She had completely missed the whole point of the binding ritual! It was designed to free Kiala — to free this young girl — from the curse that was holding her tight. And it was never going to work if Alex performed it without meaning those final words when she said them.

Alex caught Moraika's eye. Very subtly she inclined her head toward where the volcanic rock had landed. *I'll distract Kiala, you get the rock.* Moraika gave a small nod, understanding.

Alex moved across the clearing so Kiala's back was to the alpacas. She folded her arms over her chest. 'Actually ... no.'

Very slowly, Moraika started to edge toward the rock.

'Excuse me?' All of the pretend warmth from Kiala's voice was gone.

'I've changed my mind.'

'Changed your mind?' Wind swept through the clearing. Kiala did not turn around, but she screamed, 'Don't think I can't see you!'

The tigers were suddenly between Moraika and the volcanic rock, forming a circle around the black stone so the alpaca couldn't reach it. Then Kiala was right in front of Alex, her eyes blazing hate.

A hot ache flared in Alex's chest. She gasped. 'What are you doing to me!'

Uncertainty flickered through Kiala's eyes again. She frowned.

Alex clutched at her breastbone, then snatched her hand away. The hot ache was not *in* her chest, it was *on* her chest. The central stone of Grandpa Jacob's necklace pulsed hot and dark. Alex almost laughed out loud. The stone was volcanic rock!

Alex ripped the necklace over her head and grabbed the feather, pressing them against the tree. '*As pure as light I soar and swoop. From the centre I arrive, striving for havoc then sleeping forever!*'

'Stupid girl!' Kiala screamed. She turned to the tigers. 'End this! Now!'

The tigers bristled with destructive power. Alex didn't know if the alpacas would have the strength to hold them off for even another thirty seconds, but then a screech pierced the clearing, and bright white flashed in the sky above.

The white eagle streaked through the air, charging into the frontline of tigers, knocking them to the ground. She was followed by five small chicks, tiny bright cannonballs with knife-sharp beaks and claws. They ripped at the tigers' fur and nipped at their ears. The Tasmanian tigers mewled, attempting to bat the small white birds away. Kiala screamed in fury. Adrenaline and renewed energy rushed through the alpacas and, despite their lacerated coats and battered bodies, they fought on.

Alex threw the sand against the tree. '*As black as night I ebb and flow, the currents tell me where to go.*'

Then without having time to wonder if it would hurt, she grabbed Leeuie's knife from where it had fallen and sliced deep into her palm. '*An elixir of life that only the hero can bring forth*!'

Thunder and lightning ripped through the sky.

'The binding spell doesn't work!' Kiala screamed. 'And even if it did work, this tree won't hold me anymore!'

*It doesn't need to.* Alex scoured the ground until she found the tiny olive sapling she had dropped earlier.

Kiala's eyes widened. The wind fell. The battle quietened. 'Where did you get that?' she said. 'I destroyed them all. Didn't I? I destroyed them all!'

Kiala shuddered, wrapping her arms around herself. And just like that she was not an evil spirit determined to wreak vengeance on a world she thought had destroyed her. She was just a small girl. Scared. Alone. Tears pooled in her green eyes, spilling over her lashes, running down her cheeks. 'Please,' she said, her voice barely a whisper. 'I don't want to be alone again.'

'I'm sorry,' Alex said, her voice catching in her throat. And she meant it. Her heart ached for the young girl. 'I'm really sorry.' Alex closed her eyes only briefly, then plunged the blade of the knife deep into the huge olive tree. '*With love I release you from your destiny*!'

For a moment, nothing happened. But then Kiala started to glow, brighter and brighter, as though she were made of fire and stars and sunshine.

A low scream welled up from deep beneath the ground, gathering volume as it travelled through the huge, gnarled tree and burst into the sky. The tigers cowered from the sound. The alpacas tried to cover their ears, and the eagles disappeared among the trees. Alex thought her eardrums might explode, but she held the sapling high above her head. 'Come on,' she whispered under her breath. 'Come on.'

Kiala exploded into a million bright white fragments. The particles twisted around the trunk, a furious tornado of light, which was sucked inside the tree. Seconds later, a bolt of searing white heat exploded from the branches and shot straight up into the air. The column lit the stormy sky for only a second and then raced back down, directly into the sapling Alex was holding. The small tree bounced out of Alex's grip and landed on the ground. The wind fell away and the storm stopped. The forest was silent.

Alex stood, rooted to the spot. Had it worked?

She stared at the tiny olive sapling, barely daring to breathe. Around her, everything was still.

It *had* worked!

The binding ritual worked!

She'd done it!

As though waking from a dream, the Tasmanian tigers shook themselves. Very gently, they nuzzled each other, rubbing heads, touching paws. Saying hello and, as it turned out, also goodbye.

It started with one tiger. The animal lay on the forest

floor, almost smiling to itself as it closed its eyes. And then it was gone. Evaporated into a barely there waft of dust or smoke or magic. Or perhaps something else entirely.

'What just happened?' Lilly asked. 'Why did it disappear like that?'

'Kiala's gone,' Alex said, choking over the words. 'There's no magic in them anymore. Nothing keeping their bodies from being destroyed.'

'But … they can't just die!' Lilly exclaimed. 'They can't just become extinct. Again!'

Another tiger lay down. And it too was gone.

'This is what they want. They've finally found peace,' Moraika said. She moved close to the others, and they watched in respectful silence as, one by one, the rest of the tigers lay down.

Tears streamed down Alex's cheeks as each tiger sighed with relief, then vanished. Finally, they were freed from Kiala's curse. Freed from life. Freed from death.

And then, there was just one tiger left. It turned to Alex and caught her gaze. Its eyes were a deep, warm brown, and it dipped its head as if to say, *Thank you. I'm sorry.* And then it too disappeared.

A splintering crack cut through the silence as a branch from Kiala's huge old olive tree hit the ground. Another branch came crashing down, narrowly missing Leeuie, who was still unconscious. The tree was collapsing.

Alex wiped away her tears. 'We need to get out of here.'

The alpacas dragged Leeuie to the edge of the clearing, then manoeuvred him onto Alvaro's back.

Alex ducked back amongst the falling branches. She wrenched the knife out of the tree, and snatched the necklace from the ground, pulling it on. The necklace *was* good luck. The best luck.

Quickly, she grabbed the black stone bowl from her backpack. She filled it with soil from the ground and planted the tiny sapling in it. Alex had unlocked the mystery of the Amarlysa and it felt like the safest place to put the new incarnation of Kiala: the bowl made from earth and water, forged in fire and cooled by air.

'Come on,' she said. 'Let's go home.'

# CHAPTER FORTY-SIX

Snatches of clear blue sky peeked between the trees as Alex and the alpacas made the journey back to Grandpa Jacob's. Birds darted about, calling to each other, and a light breeze wafted through the leaves, carrying scents of eucalyptus and moss and warm earth.

Alex walked in stunned silence, cradling the bowl containing the small olive sapling to her chest. She still couldn't quite believe the binding ritual had actually worked.

The alpacas were battle-weary and wounded, but moved through the forest with lightness and ease. Kiala was no danger to them anymore. They could go back to a life of afternoon naps and apples.

Everything had worked out. Soon, they would be back at the farm. Grandpa Jacob would know what to do about the still-unconscious Leeuie, and Mum would be awake. They would make a pot of tea and a huge plate of Alexandwiches and Alex would tell Mum just how much she'd missed her and how much she loved her. Alex didn't tell her that enough. And maybe not today, but someday soon, Alex would phone Dad.

Lilly's voice cut through her thoughts. 'Leeuie's hand just moved!'

They all stopped walking, and stared intently at Leeuie's fingers. His body remained completely motionless, draped over Alvaro like a human saddlecloth.

'You imagined it,' Ollin said after a few seconds.

'I didn't!'

'Well, he's not moving now, is he?'

Leeuie's hand twitched.

Lilly rounded on Ollin, triumphant. 'I told you so!'

'Leeuie?' Alex helped lower him to the ground. 'Are you awake?'

Leeuie let out a pained groan and his eyelids snapped open. Then, as though he had been plugged into an electrical socket, his whole body began to jerk and spasm. Breath gargled in his throat and his eyes rolled back in his head so only the whites were showing.

Ollin took a skittish step backwards. 'What's happening to him?'

Alex had no idea. She caught hold of Leeuie's shoulders, trying to still his shuddering body. 'Leeuie? Can you hear me?'

Leeuie stopped thrashing. His arms flopped by his side and his head lolled to the right. The colour started to drain from him, like water from a bath. First from his fingers, then his palm, and all the way up his arm until the whole limb was a pale blueish white, the freckles an odd grey.

Alex wasn't a doctor, but she was pretty sure this wasn't a normal symptom of being hit on the head. And Kiala was gone, so it couldn't be her doing this to him. So why was it happening?

She frantically rubbed Leeuie's fingers, trying to make the colour come back. His hand was ice cold, the skin pitted and rough from the countless splinters and nicks. She noticed the splinter he had gotten yesterday while they were in the forest. A dark sliver of wood wedged into the fatty part of his palm, at the base of the thumb.

Alex gasped.

The splinter. Leeuie still had a tiny piece of Kiala's old tree in him.

She dived for her backpack, fumbling through the contents until she found Leeuie's knife.

'Sorry Leeuie,' she mumbled, 'this is going to hurt.'

She pressed the sharp edge of the knife into his palm, slicing through the top level of skin and down to the muscle. She worked the tip of the knife underneath the splinter, just like Leeuie had done for her, and flicked it out.

For the longest moment nothing happened, but then the colour rushed back to Leeuie's body and he sat straight up, gasping lungfuls of air.

'Alex? What are you doing here?' He blinked and peered around, confused. 'What am I doing here?'

Alex exhaled the breath she didn't realise she'd been holding. Her face split into a gigantic grin. 'It's a *really* long story.'

Moraika peered at the splinter Alex had dug from Leeuie's hand. 'It was from Kiala's tree?'

Alex nodded. 'Without Kiala the tree can't live anymore. I guess anything infected by the wood is also —' She stopped talking abruptly. She remembered the splinters of wood stuck between the tigers' teeth. She thought of how easily one of those splinters might be transferred through a single bite. Of how it could get stuck in a wound. And how that tiny fragment of Kiala's tree could right now be draining the life out of Mum. Panic flooded Alex's entire body. She leaped up, her pulse exploding in her ears. 'I need to get home. Now!'

No one questioned her. 'Go,' Moraika said. 'We'll meet you there.'

Alex scrambled onto Alvaro and clutched around his neck as they thundered away.

At the farm, Alex burst through the kitchen door and raced into Mum's room, her heart pounding. *Please don't let me be too late … Please don't let me be too late …*

Grandpa Jacob was sitting on the bed, eyes wide and frightened, clutching Mum's hand. The colour had already drained from her body and Mum was white as death.

'I need tweezers!' Alex cried.

Grandpa Jacob seemed paralysed with shock. 'She just started shaking and …'

Alex heaved Grandpa Jacob to standing and pushed him toward the door. 'Tweezers! Now!'

She tore at the bandage wrapped around Mum's arm and twisted the bedside light so it was shining directly onto the cut. The wound was raw, but there was no blood. Mum's chest shuddered with a shaky breath, then stilled. 'No!' Alex shouted. 'You're not allowed to die!'

Grandpa Jacob limped quickly back in with a pair of metal tweezers.

Alex grabbed them, then leaned down close to the wound, examining each of the individual puncture marks. 'Where are you?' she muttered, gingerly prodding deep under the skin.

There it was! A tiny piece of wood, no longer than her fingernail. She pushed the tweezers into the flesh and wrenched the splinter out.

Alex stared at Mum's face. *Come on, come on …* She barely realised she was doing it, but under her breath she started to sing. It was the song that Mum had sung to her at the bottom of the lake. The song Mum always used to sing when Alex was sick. The song that was supposed to save Mum's life.

*As pure as light I soar and swoop,*
*From the centre I arrive, striving for havoc then sleeping forever.*
*As black as night I ebb and flow, the currents tell me where to go.*
*An elixir of life that only the hero can bring forth.*
*With love I release you from your destiny.*

Mum inhaled sharply then sat bolt upright. Her eyes focused on Alex. 'Hello sweetheart.' Her voice was weak. She looked around, then frowned. 'Is this my old bedroom?'

Alex couldn't decide if she wanted to laugh or cry, so she settled for doing both. She flew at Mum, wrapping both arms around her neck.

'Alex? What's the matter?'

'Nothing,' Alex cry-laughed. 'Absolutely nothing!'

Mum winced as she tried to hug Alex. She looked in surprise at the injury on her arm. 'When did I do this?'

Alex wiped away her tears and let out a loud sigh. Where to begin? 'Well, you were —'

From behind Alex, Grandpa Jacob cleared his throat. She hesitated. Right. As if Mum would actually believe this story. 'You, er, had a really bad flu. And you tripped.'

'And now we'd better get your arm cleaned up,' Grandpa Jacob said. 'I'll get some antiseptic and a bandage.'

He turned to leave the room, but not before Alex and Mum saw tears flooding out of his eyes.

'Dad? Are you … crying?'

He dragged the back of his hand across his cheek. 'Of course not!'

'For goodness sake,' Mum muttered, smiling shyly at him, 'it was just the flu.'

# CHAPTER FORTY-SEVEN

Alex padded through the kitchen and out to the back garden, where Mum and Grandpa Jacob were drinking tea and watching the shadows lengthen across the valley. They had been doing a lot of that over the last few days. Just sitting. Watching the day unfold in front of them.

Mum's memories from when she was sick were pretty hazy (although, she did remember having a *very* vivid dream about a Tasmanian tiger), but her strength was slowly returning and, all in all, she was back to being regular old Mum. Which was, in Alex's opinion, the best and most perfect Mum there ever was.

Alex nestled on the bench next to her and gazed over the charred olive grove, where tiny seedlings had miraculously managed to push through the ash, bringing drops of colour to the charcoal ground. Alex wasn't sure if Mum totally bought Grandpa Jacob's explanation that he had burned the trees to help them grow back stronger, but she hadn't pressed him on it.

Mum handed Alex a slice of apple cake. Leeuie had dropped it over an hour earlier, freshly-baked and still warm from the oven. Yesterday had been apple strudel, and the day before apple muffins. His way of saying, 'Sorry I tried to kill you but thanks for saving my life anyway'.

Alex had told him, over and over, that he didn't have anything to be sorry for. Especially seeing as he'd already saved *her* life. And, besides, what were friends for if not getting rid of the evil spirits possessing you? But she didn't protest too much because what kind of person turns down baked goods as great as these?

'Did you get through to your dad?' Mum asked, stealing a bite of Alex's cake.

Alex nodded. The day before, Grandpa Jacob had insisted Alex and Leeuie accompany him into town so he could buy 'one of those Inter Web things' so they could easily keep in touch.

'Just for any Kiala developments,' he'd added. 'I'm not one of those people who needs to chitchat every day about the weather and what I'm having for dinner.'

'Sure,' Alex said, suppressing a grin. She suspected she would have many video calls with Grandpa Jacob in her not-too-distant future on topics such as the weather and what he was having for dinner. Not that she minded. In fact, she was quite looking forward to it.

Alex had also taken the opportunity of Grandpa Jacob getting with the digital program to make things right with

Dad and (virtually) meet her little sister for the first time.

'So?' Mum raised an eyebrow. 'What's the verdict?'

Alex snuggled closer to Mum as the sun dipped lower and the sky over the farm burned brilliant shades of orange and pink. 'She is the most hilarious little sister ever,' she said. 'Dad was trying to make her do this gurgling noise that he thinks sounds like a blocked drain, but then she puked all over him and he started swearing, and then Courtney —' she added the obligatory eyeroll here, more out of habit than anything else, because Dad's girlfriend was alright really, '— started swearing at him for swearing in front of his daughters.'

Mum laughed. 'I bet he's looking forward to seeing you next week.'

Alex was looking forward to seeing him, too. Being mad at someone for so long was exhausting. Not that she was going to admit that, of course. She was fairly confident she'd be able to milk this for more than a few ice-cream sundae dinners.

Grandpa Jacob cleared his throat. 'And I suppose, Elina, you'll be heading back to work after Alex leaves?'

'I was actually wondering about staying a while longer,' Mum said. 'Just in case you need help with anything.'

'Oh, well,' Grandpa Jacob blustered, 'I don't need the help —'

'Of course you don't,' Alex and Mum said at the same time.

Grandpa Jacob shot them a look. 'But it's no bother if you want your old room back for a few days. Or weeks. Alex, that goes for you, too. You're welcome anytime.' He fiddled with his mug. 'If you want to come back, that is.'

Alex grinned at him. 'Wild alpacas couldn't keep me away.'

***

Down in the paddock, the alpacas shook grass from themselves and made their way to the barn. Moraika's neck wound was healing well, thanks to Leeuie's Discovery Channel inspired medical skills, and he'd since added 'vet' alongside 'farmer', 'explorer' and 'botanist' to the list of things he wanted to be when he grew up.

'Come on, Ollin,' Moraika called to the black alpaca who was still staring, mesmerised, at the huge pile of apples Alex and Leeuie had surprised them with that morning. 'They're not going to grow legs and walk away overnight!'

'They're just so beautiful I can barely breathe!' Ollin called back.

Alex had to cover her laugh with a cough. She gave Moraika a secret wave and the alpaca lifted a foot, waving back.

Mum squinted, leaning forward. 'Huh,' she said. 'If I didn't know better, I would have sworn that alpaca just waved at us.'

'Maybe she did,' Alex said.

# EPILOGUE

The olive sapling rested on the windowsill in the kitchen. All the doors and windows were closed, but the tree's tiny leaves twitched as though caught by the breeze.

From inside her new prison, Kiala's recent memories flooded back. She bristled with anger, making the sapling shudder and twitch more. She was trapped. Alone and weak.

Again.

She pressed at the corners of the magic binding her, testing it. It was strong, but … this time, something felt different.

Something *was* different.

Her sister. She could feel a connection to her sister. As fragile as the single strand of a new spider's web, but it was there.

Kiala did not know where on this abysmal earth her twin sister's spirit was. They had been separated so long ago by geography, physics … by forces so powerful they did not even have names. She didn't want to remember her. She didn't want to think of her. It was Resila's fault she was here, after all. Her fault she was all alone. Her fault she was not alive, not dead.

And yet …

*Sister, are you there?*

Her whisper latched onto the wind, flew over mountains and across oceans. Thousands of miles away, the earth shuddered. Trees shook, and the sandy desert floor rippled and bowed. The small earthquake would not even make the evening news. These things happened all the time over here.

But Kiala knew better.

*Sister. There you are.*

As suddenly as it had started, the little olive sapling in Tasmania stopped swaying and sat motionless on the windowsill once more.

*I'm coming, sister. I'm coming for you.*

# Acknowledgements

There are so many people who have helped bring this book to life.

All the fine folks at Fremantle Press, especially Cate Sutherland for her masterful edits. You have made this a better story.

My writers group, the Webster Wordsmiths, with special thanks to Melina and Shana, who must have read this book almost as many times as I have.

All my pals at the Castro Writers' Coop in San Francisco who cheered me on through those early morning writing sessions, the lovely humans at Paper Bird Books in Fremantle who were fabulous company during my writer's residency, and all my early readers who provided thoughtful and encouraging feedback — thank you. You know who you are.

To my aunts-in-law, Grit and Tru, for letting me outstay my welcome on the alpaca farm in Tasmania where the idea for this story was born.

My wonderful family (of whom there are too many to name!), but particularly Mike, Joy, Lucy, Rich, Sus and Sal.

And finally, Khrob, who actually took me seriously all those years ago when I said, 'I think I want to write a book …'

# About the Author

Kathryn writes novels, screenplays, articles — and the occasional shopping list. She has a PhD in marketing, several screenwriting credits, and her stories have appeared in magazines, journals and online. She spends way too much time in conversation with imaginary characters, and not-so-secretly wishes she lived in a dance movie.

A catalogue record for this
book is available from the
National Library of Australia

Fremantle Press is supported by the State Government through
the Department of Local Government, Sport and Cultural Industries.

 Department of
Local Government, Sport
and Cultural Industries